Freelance

On The Galactic Tunnel Network

Freelance

On The Galactic
Tunnel Network

Foner Books

ISBN 978-1-948691-23-9

Copyright 2020 by E. M. Foner

Northampton, Massachusetts

One

"Let me make sure I have this straight," Walter said to the young reporter. "You're not willing to write about food anymore, but you're not resigning from the paper."

"Now you've got it," Georgia said, beaming a smile at the managing editor of the Galactic Free Press. "So we're all set?"

"Wait. Please, take a seat. I'm still a little lost here."

"It's simple. When I first came to work at the paper I was told that everybody has to pay their dues before they can choose their own assignments. Now I've paid my dues and I'm ready to become an investigative journalist."

"I admire your enthusiasm, but we have a system in place," Walter told her. "I know I say that my door is always open, but you're supposed to start by bringing new story ideas to your section editor, and then the two of you would present together to the editorial board. We take investigative journalism very seriously."

"That's why I want to do it," Georgia said, making it sound like the managing editor had just stated the most obvious fact in the world. "If there's nothing else..."

"But you can't just declare yourself an investigative journalist!"

"Why not? I have a four-year degree in journalism from the New University System on Earth."

"And we agreed to overlook that particular shortcoming in your background when we gave you a job. Most of our employees get their start writing for student papers via their teacher bots or reporting on the Children's News Network. In many cases, we've already picked up some of their stories through syndication before they even apply here. Our publisher prefers hands-on experience, but I have a soft spot for Earth degrees since I was educated there myself."

"It's not my fault I grew up without a teacher bot," Georgia said. "My parents are anti-alien and they sent me to the commune school. I earned a full scholarship to the New University based on the competitive entrance exams."

"Yes, and I'm sure that played into our decision to give you a chance, but all of this is beside the point. We try to give our staff the maximum flexibility in determining their work/life balance, but when it comes to reporting, I'm afraid that we're sticklers for insisting our employees write the stories they're assigned. The Galactic Free Press is like a giant puzzle," Walter continued with one of his favorite analogies. "We have over a hundred section editors managing thousands of reporters to provide the information our readers have come to expect. You're being paid to report on the local food scene, and if you want to run off and do something else, we'll have to transfer your salary to whoever steps up and takes your place."

"That makes perfect sense. After all, investigative journalism must pay better than food writing."

Walter massaged his temples and fought against the urge to put his head down on his desk and simply wait for the young reporter to leave him in peace.

2

"We don't have an open slot for an investigative journalist at the moment, but I'd be happy to add you to the list of candidates."

"No, I want to start now," Georgia insisted. "I left Earth three years ago and I haven't been off Union Station since I got here. There are large human populations spread across hundreds of worlds and alien orbitals around the tunnel network, but the farthest I've ever traveled to report a story is the distance from the nearest lift tube to a restaurant. The most exciting assignment I've had since taking this job was sampling tribute recipes for the All Species Cookbook."

"But you're not quitting?"

"Of course not," Georgia said, looking shocked at the idea. "I've worked hard to get where I am."

"So you'll talk this over with your section editor..."

"My editor told me to come and see you."

"I understand," Walter said, glancing towards the grandfather clock in the corner as if he hoped that time would run out and save him. "So you aren't willing to do your job anymore, but you still want to work for us?"

"Right. I'm going to investigate financial fraud. Ever since I read that series of articles about the retired folks who got scammed on Flower, I've been spending all of my free time studying up on the history of financial crimes in a self-directed Open University extension course. Libby says that I'm ready."

"The Stryx station librarian told you to change jobs?"

"Well, she might have said that I'm as ready as I'll ever be, but it amounts to the same thing," Georgia insisted. "I'm not leaving this office until you agree."

"It just doesn't work that way. What's this big story you want to investigate?"

"Colony One. The whole thing is a scam. I can feel it in my bones."

"I'm sorry, I'm not sure I heard you correctly," Walter said. "You want to investigate Colony One?"

"Exactly. Humans have been going out on alien-owned colony ships as contract workers for decades, and with Flower, we have a Dollnick colony ship working for us, even if she just goes around in a great big circle visiting sovereign human communities. But purchasing a colony ship for ourselves would cost more than humanity is worth."

"Their goal is to buy a scrapped ship and refurbish it in an alien shipyard. They have the backing of EarthCent, and coincidentally, Colony One advertises their meetings in our paper."

"Are you saying I can't move into investigative journalism because Colony One sponsors the free edition?"

"Now you're conflating two different subjects," Walter protested. "Let me make this as simple for you as possible. If you're willing to report the stories your section editor assigns, then you're welcome to continue working for us as a full-time employee. If you need to go off and do your own thing, I suggest you take a leave of absence, or change your status to freelance and—"

"How would that work?" Georgia interrupted.

"Well, since you've reached three years of employment with us, we would allow you to keep your press credentials, your translation implant, and your programmable cred. You would be assigned to the freelance desk, which would pay you for any stories they accept."

"That's what I want," Georgia said, getting up again. "I'm available to start right away."

"Freelancers are always available to start right away, it's the nature of the business," Walter told her. He rose as well and offered her a handshake. "I wish you the best, and I'll be watching for your byline."

"Thank you. Could I ask what it pays?"

"The freelance editors have leeway in determining compensation, but in recognition of the fact that you are paying your own expenses, the per-story rate is appreciably higher than what our full-time reporters earn on a prorated basis."

"Can I get an advance?"

"I'm afraid that advances are only available to freelancers who establish a track record with the paper."

"But I've been working for you three years," she protested.

"A track record as a freelancer. If you intend to travel in pursuit of your story, the freelance desk may be willing to offer a partial subsidy if you're willing to write about the local cuisine."

Georgia left the managing editor's office, and after consulting with the receptionist, made her way through the cubicle maze to a group of desks in the corner of the large space occupied by the Galactic Free Press. Something that looked like an old harpoon was suspended from the ceiling, and a sign hanging from the shaft read, "Freelance Desk."

"Hello?" she called, looking around the area, which appeared to be empty. "Anybody here?"

"Right behind you," a voice announced, and Georgia turned to see a silver-haired man with a mug of coffee in one hand and a sticky bun in the other. "I'm Roland. How can I help you?"

"Georgia," she said, offering a hand, and then realizing that he couldn't reciprocate. "Sorry. I'm here about becoming a freelancer."

Roland glanced at the Galactic Free Press ID hanging from a lanyard around her neck and snorted. "Another one, huh? What is it this time? War? Sports?"

"I don't understand."

The man set down his sticky bun, half-sat on the desktop next to it, and took a sip of his coffee before responding. "Have you been through the kidnap avoidance training course?"

"I graduated last year," Georgia said. "I have a certificate somewhere if you need to see it."

"And are you double-dipping from EarthCent Intelligence?" he asked suspiciously.

"No. I've been working as a food writer the last three years but I'm ready to become an investigative journalist. Walter said you might give me an advance if I commit to turning in food stories from the places I visit. Why did you think I worked for EarthCent Intelligence?"

"We get spies in here all the time hoping to use the paper as cover while collecting a salary from two employers," Roland explained, then took another sip from his coffee. "I'll have to talk with your section editor, but I suspect we can do something for you. Food articles always pull good read rates. What's the big story you're working on?"

"I'm going to investigate Colony One," Georgia said proudly.

"Nothing there," the freelance editor told her. "Still, if you're planning on following them around to their local seminars, you'll learn something about chasing down leads that may come in handy later."

"Why is everybody so sure that it's not a scam? They're raising an enormous amount of money to buy and recondition a colony ship from one of the human-sized species."

"But they're only taking pledges," Roland pointed out. "The first phase is to get enough funds committed for the aliens to take them seriously, and only then will they try to negotiate a price and a shipyard lease. Colony ships aren't two-man traders, you know. Between technology transfer issues, resident artificial intelligence, and the fact that the tunnel network might go a thousand years at a stretch without seeing a colony ship retired, it doesn't strike me as a promising field for scammers."

"That's what makes it perfect," Georgia insisted. "Nobody expects anything to come of it anytime soon, but the promoters must be paying themselves salaries and travel expenses. The scam is that by keeping the focus on sums in the trillions, they can skim off millions and nobody will ever think twice about it."

"Nobody but you. My gut tells me that you're off base on this, but the whole point of going freelance is that you can do what you want with your time. When are you planning on leaving?"

"I have to arrange for transportation, and whatever advance you can pay me for food stories will play into my plans. I have three years of savings, but it hasn't been cheap living here."

"I admire the conviction of youth. You're what? Twenty-five?"

"My birthday is today. Becoming an investigative journalist is my present to myself."

"Check back in with me tomorrow and we'll see what we can do about that advance, but don't expect instant riches. The most we ever extend to employees who go freelance amounts to a cycle's pay."

"I'll take what I can get. Thank you."

Georgia practically skipped out of the main office, where she'd been sharing a cubicle with several other beat reporters ever since being assigned to food writing, and made a beeline for the nearest lift tube.

"Tunnel Trips spaceship rentals, the place that advertises in the paper," she instructed the conveyance. A thought struck her as the capsule began to move. "Do you think I needed to make a reservation first, Libby?"

"Due to the relatively small size of the rental fleet, reserving in advance is the best way to assure availability for the dates you require," the Stryx station librarian responded. "How long are you planning to be away?"

"I don't know, as long as it takes, I guess. You're the one who told me that if I want to chase all over the galaxy in pursuit of a story, I may as well get started."

"If that's what you heard. Will you be keeping your apartment?"

"Yes, of course. It's the only home I have."

"If you're leaving for an extended period, you'll be paying for a space you aren't using, and I expect your finances will be tight."

"Yes, but what else can I do?"

"We provide a storage service for long-term renters and you recently qualified. I can send bots to clean out your apartment and put everything in storage at a cost of ten percent of your current rent, plus a one-time fee of fifty creds for moving expenses. You can contact me from anywhere with a return date, and I'll have your things installed in a new apartment before you arrive."

"All of that for fifty creds plus ten percent of my regular rent?"

"Ten percent per cycle," the station librarian explained. "The fee is ongoing, but I can have it taken out of your security deposit, though you'll have to replenish the reserve when you return."

"That would set me up for more than a year. I'll do it," Georgia said. The doors opened on a familiar corridor and she stepped out of the capsule. "Hey. This is where I took my kidnap avoidance training."

"Mac's Bones," Libby continued the conversation over the reporter's implant. "The leaseholder sublets space for training to EarthCent Intelligence, and he also has a small-ship campground, plus the new rental agency. The kiosk isn't far from the entrance."

A minute later, Georgia found herself standing at a small counter manned by a cheerful Horten girl whose mood was apparent from her brown skin.

"Welcome to Tunnel Trips. I'm Marilla and I'll be your agent. Do you have a reservation, Miss?"

"Georgia Hunt. I don't, actually. Are all of those ships taken?" she asked, gesturing in the direction of the parking area.

"The three ships with full advertising wraps are the only rentals, the rest are here for repairs or are taking advantage of the camping facility and chandlery."

"But with three to choose from, my not having a reservation won't be a problem."

"We do book most of our rentals in advance so I'll have to check the schedule," Marilla said apologetically. "I know that two of the ships are already spoken for tomorrow, so unless you're only going somewhere overnight..."

"I don't know how long I'll be gone. Months, I think."

"Months?"

"Sorry, I meant a cycle or more."

"I understand Humanese, it's just that we've never done such a long-term rental before," the Horten girl said. "We only started the business recently."

"Will long-term be less expensive than renting by the day? I couldn't afford the daily rate I've seen advertised."

"Seventy-nine creds a day, not including optional Thark insurance, which is another ten creds a day. How much were you hoping to pay?"

"Are we bargaining now?"

"To be honest, we've never discussed the possibility of open-ended rentals. The ships are single-cabin craft, as you can see, without any cargo capacity. You can't take them off the tunnel network, and they certainly aren't capable of landing on a planet, so we mainly rent them to business-men who are looking for an alternative to multi-stop trips on commercial liners."

"I'll be staying on the tunnel network, I think," Georgia said. "But seventy-nine creds a day is more than I earn when I'm working full-time. I was hoping it would be closer to what I'm going to save on rent while I'm not here."

"Do you have experience living in Zero-G?"

"Just the time it took to get from the space elevator hub at Earth to the liner I took to come out here. I got pretty sick."

"What is the purpose of your rental?"

"I'm a reporter for the Galactic Free Press. I'm investigating a story, but I'll also be sending in regular pieces about local food culture."

"Let me—Mr. McAllister?" Marilla called, waving to an older man in coveralls who was walking a dog the size of a small pony. "Could you come here a minute?"

"Isn't that the ambassador's husband?" Georgia asked in a hushed voice. "I don't want to make trouble for anybody."

"In addition to holding the lease on Mac's Bones, he's a part-owner in Tunnel Trips and has a lot of experience in space travel," the Horten girl told Georgia. "Plus, he's really friendly."

"Joe McAllister," the owner of Mac's Bones introduced himself, offering Georgia a handshake. "Beowulf acts as if he knows you."

"Georgia Hunt. I met Beowulf last year when I was taking the kidnap avoidance course for Galactic Free Press reporters. I used to share my lunch with him."

"No surprise there. Did you have a question about one of the advanced courses? Thomas and Chance are at an intelligence conference, but I saw Judith around here earlier, and she could probably help," Joe said, looking back in the direction of the training camp.

"Georgia is interested in a long-term rental, Mr. McAllister," Marilla said. "Like, indefinite."

"We don't have a rule against it if there's a ship available, but I can't imagine it's the best option. Where are you going?"

"That's just it, I'm not sure yet," Georgia replied. "I'm an investigative journalist, or I will be as soon as I leave Union Station, and I don't know where the story will take me. I plan to catch up with the Colony One people and follow them for a while."

"Doing that in a rental would get expensive in a hurry," Joe said doubtfully. "I have a friend who keeps a two-man

11

trader she's not using in the Stryx stasis lot. Lynx is currently serving as the third officer on Flower, so she'd probably be willing to rent it to you as long as you could put down a security deposit and buy Thark insurance. How much piloting experience do you have?"

"None, and I doubt I'd be able to afford a security deposit for anything like that. I'm a freelancer. I was hoping that I'd get a big discount on the rental for taking it long term."

"How much of a discount?"

"Whatever it would take to make the price the same as what I'll be saving by not paying rent for my apartment."

"Which is?"

"Three hundred and twenty creds a cycle."

"I'm sorry," Joe told her. "Maybe we could stretch a rental to a week for that if things were slow here, but it wouldn't make any sense for us to go longer."

"I can't give up before I even start," Georgia said in frustration. "What if I rented a ship one way, turned it in as soon as I arrived, and then rented another one when I was ready to move on to the next stop?"

"I know the Colony One people travel in their own ship because I've seen it in the news. That means they can go places on the tunnel network where we don't have any franchises yet, so you'd be out of luck."

"How much of a security deposit do you think your friend would require? If I can sell the paper enough food stories from the places I stop to cover my expenses, I could come up with two thousand creds," Georgia offered, naming an amount equaling more than half of her savings.

Joe shook his head. "That idea went out the airlock when you told me you don't have any piloting experience, and the security deposit would have been twenty times that amount." He hesitated a moment, then asked, "Have you considered negotiating a ride with a trader?"

"How would that help? Don't traders have places they need to go to deliver cargo?"

"Some take consignments, but most traders carry their own inventory and lay out the blanket wherever they find themselves. A solo trader might take on a passenger to earn a little ready money and have somebody to talk to for a change."

"And you think I could find a trader who would be willing to follow the Colony One seminar around?"

"If you come back after supper I can introduce you to a trader I know," Joe said. "Nice guy, usually stops in here a few times a year. It wouldn't be right for me to discuss his business, but he probably wouldn't turn up his nose at a little extra income."

Two

"Grains," Larry swore, dropping the ratchet wrench and rubbing his knuckles, which had slammed into the fuel pack when the five-point Sharf socket slipped off the bolt. He grimaced in disgust at the pink socket and pulled it off the ratchet to check it again on the bolt head. The telltale movement proved it was a size too large. "Three shades of red, three shades of blue—why can't the Sharf number their sockets like normal aliens?"

"Need a hand under there?" a voice called.

"I could use the middle red socket, or maybe it's dark pink." A colored socket rolled into the tight space where Larry was working on his back. He snagged it on the move and tried it on the bolt head. "Perfect." Larry mounted the socket on the ratchet, set the torque, and quickly made up the four bolts. Then he wormed his way out from under the ship and was surprised to see a man and a woman, both dressed in matching slacks and blazers.

"Are you the owner?" the woman asked him. "I'm Marcie Haynes, and this is my partner, Jim Silver."

"Larry, no last name. Thanks for the socket, but if you're selling something, I don't have any cash to spare."

"We're here to give you money, Larry," Jim said, flashing a broad smile. "We're with MORE, the financial services company that cares more. You probably received a notice about your ship's mortgage changing hands."

"No, I didn't hear anything about that." Larry rose to his feet and wiped his hands on the rag he kept tied around a belt loop while doing maintenance work. "I bought this ship directly from the Sharf and financed it through them."

"And they recently sold us a pool of securitized mortgages taken out by humans for pre-owned ships."

"I would have remembered agreeing to a change in terms."

"Nothing has changed except that your payments are now routed to us. Your original mortgage contract terms will remain in force throughout the loan period, which in your case," Marcie said, glancing down at a large-screen tab, "will be another seven years. Unless, of course, you choose to refinance."

"And we can offer you generous refi terms," Jim jumped in. "Given the large down payment you made and the relatively short term of your loan, you've got a lot of equity built up in this beauty that we can help you access. How does fifty thousand creds cash sound to you?"

"I don't understand," Larry said. "You want me to take a second mortgage on my ship?"

"Think of it as a business improvement loan, or better yet, simply reclaiming your own money, because that equity is something you've worked hard to earn," the woman told him. "According to our data you've never missed a payment, so you'll qualify for our best interest rate."

"My father helped me make the down payment on the condition that I never borrow against it," Larry said. "Thank you for the help with the socket and coming all the way down here, but I'm looking forward to the day the ship is mine, free and clear."

15

"Message received," Jim said with an insincere grin, and placed a hand on his heart.

"We aren't just here to offer you a refi," Marcie continued, tapping and swiping at her tab. "Take a look at this."

"MORE wants to see all of our customers succeed, so we've put together a number of new tools for collaboration," Jim said, as Larry studied the display. "There's a built-in rating system that allows affiliated traders to grade each other's contributions so you can build a reputation. I know you're thinking that the whole point of being an independent trader is going it alone, but—"

"I already have a reputation," Larry cut him off, handing back the tab. "I appreciate the offer, but I once subscribed to the Raider/Trader platform the Verlocks maintain, and though I earned steady money, it made me feel like I was running a delivery service. I grew up in a trading family, third generation, and I'm not in it just to squeeze every last cred out of my cargo."

"Oh well, we can't force you," Marcie said, slipping the tab back into her shoulder bag. "If you change your mind, any MORE rep can provide you with a free tab and set up your credentials."

"You're a hard sell, Larry," Jim added, but his smile didn't reach his eyes. "Our goal is to become the top financial services partner for independent traders, so don't be surprised when you find that all of your friends are availing themselves of our services."

Larry watched the pair of sales reps head towards the other two-man Sharf trader currently parked in Mac's Bones and wondered just how many mortgages MORE had acquired. Then he saw Joe McAllister walking towards him with a slender brunette, and for a second he thought that the ambassador's husband had found a customer for the ten thousand air-tight salad containers he was hoping to unload for cash. Then he saw her press ID and realized she wasn't a buyer.

"Evening, Larry," Joe greeted him. "Did you get that fuel pack bolted up without a problem?"

"Fit like a glove. Thanks for welding on the adapter bracket for me. I might have burned a hole in the pack if I tried welding it myself, but I couldn't afford the exact replacement size."

"Sharf fuel packs are practically indestructible. They build them that way so you can't disassemble it and replace the catalyst yourself." Joe ushered the reporter forward and continued with a simple introduction. "Georgia, this is Larry. Larry, Georgia is trying to find a ride. She has a peculiar travel itinerary and renting a ship from Tunnel Trips wouldn't make financial sense for her."

"Pleased to meet you, Larry," the reporter said, shaking the trader's calloused hand. "Joe told me you might consider a passenger?"

"It's not out of the question," Larry replied. "I don't have any commitments to be anywhere for the next few weeks, and I was going to check the trade section in the Galactic Free Press and see what looked promising. You're a full-time reporter?"

"I was. As of today, I'm a freelance investigative journalist, though I'll be writing some local food articles to pay the bills."

"I'll just leave you two to talk then," Joe said. "I can vouch for Larry and his family, Georgia. They're good people, been stopping here since I opened the place. If Larry takes you on, don't forget to stock up at the chandlery. It's run by my son-in-law."

"He's a great old guy," Larry told Georgia as soon as Joe was out of earshot. "Most places rent tools, but everything here comes free with the camp rental, and Joe's a genius at tracking down replacement parts. So where do you need to go?"

"I'm working on a story about the Colony One movement and I want to follow them around for a while. You know, see what kind of people show up at their events, whether they present everybody with the same story, that sort of thing."

"And you can get paid for that?"

"It depends on whether the paper wants to buy what I write, but I have some savings, and they'll pay me per article to keep writing food stories."

"So how much were you looking to spend?"

"I'm giving up my apartment and I was hoping to keep my transportation costs to something like a rent payment. Or maybe I could work my way?"

"Cash on the barrelhead," Larry said. "I have a mortgage payment to make, and the truth is, I've got more merchandise than ready money."

"Would fifty creds a week help?"

"One cred a week would help, but that doesn't mean it would be worth sharing my living space and chasing around after the Colony One people. How about a hundred?"

"I don't really have any experience with the whole trading culture thing so I don't want to get in a haggling war with you. Would seventy-five work?"

"You're better at negotiating than you think," Larry said. "Come aboard and take a look around before we shake on the deal because you may want to change your mind. Have you ever traveled on a small ship?"

"No, but I'm not claustrophobic," she said, following him up the ramp. "And it's a lot larger than my apartment."

"The fat part of a trade ship is cargo space. The skinny end is where we live."

"Oh." Georgia paused as they entered the cargo hold, which fit between the technical deck and the bridge, and waited a moment for her eyes to adjust. "You use cargo netting in space?"

"Can't have the goods floating around in Zero-G, and stackable containers are too inefficient in terms of the limited storage space on a small ship like this. Cargo netting is flexible. We take the ladder to the left there."

"No stairs?"

"Some larger trade ships have a companionway, which is like very steep stairs, but a ladder makes the best use of space unless you can afford a field lift."

"What's that?" Georgia asked when they reached the ladder. "You go first, I'm wearing a skirt."

"All of the advanced species have mastered various levels of field manipulation technology," Larry explained over his shoulder as he climbed the ladder. "Even the Drazens and the Hortens can manage the atmosphere retention field generators that make it possible for ships to enter docking bays without a giant airlock. The older species can do much fancier stuff, like autoparking ships with manipulator fields, or on a smaller scale, lifting crew from the cargo deck to the bridge. And don't plan on wearing skirts during the trip. They aren't practical in Zero-G."

"So we'll be living on the bridge?" Georgia asked as she climbed through the open hatch behind him. "What are all of those machines on the ceiling?"

19

"Stationary bike, rock climbing machine, rowing," Larry pointed to the exercise equipment in rapid sequence. "We've got magnetic fields to protect us from the worst types of radiation, but if you don't exercise every day in Zero-G, your muscles start shrinking in a hurry."

"But how can you ride a bike upside down?"

"You really are a newbie, aren't you. There is no upside down when you're weightless. See the harness hanging by elastic straps from the treadmill? That's what keeps me in place when I'm running."

"Oh, right. I wasn't thinking. So we sleep in the chairs?"

"In Zero-G, I just tether off to an ankle and float. When we're parked on a spinning station or a planet, I string a hammock, and I have a spare."

"The bathroom is behind there?" Georgia asked, pointing at the fanfold door pulled across a nook created by a section of storage lockers along the back of the curved bulkhead.

"Right. I can let you have one of those lockers for your clothes and another for food. You'll be responsible for your own eats. The chandlery is a good place to stock up, and Kevin, the guy who runs it, was a trader himself. He can tell you what you'll need."

"And you'll be willing to drop whatever you're doing and follow the Colony One people when they move to their next stop?"

"It's not like we need to tail the ship. They publish their schedule a cycle in advance. It's in your paper," he added, pointing at her press ID.

"I know that. I just mean, can I trust you not to get hung up on a deal somewhere and start ignoring me? I may not have any experience as a trader, but I know a little about guys."

20

"And I know a little more than I'd like about gals," Larry shot back. "Maybe it would be best for both of us if we take it a week at a time."

"Deal," Georgia said, and the two shook hands for the second time in ten minutes. "When do you need the first seventy-five creds?"

"Now would be good. I was going to try stretching the filters for an extra cycle, but with another person on board, I may as well change them while I'm here and can get them for a good price."

"Air filters?"

"Air and sanitary water. You're in luck with me because I traded for a Dollnick Zero-G shower a couple of years back, uses some advanced field technology to keep the water contained and moving. You wouldn't want to drink it even with the filter, though I've heard of some traders having to do that in emergencies."

"I think I'll buy extra water." Georgia fished in her purse and came up with the programmable cred the Galactic Free Press provided all employees to make their payroll. "Can you take it out of this, or do you need cash?"

"I've got a mini-register, all independent traders do," Larry told her, accepting the coin. He opened one of the storage lockers next to the bathroom and removed the alien device. Then he inserted her programmable cred, entered the amount, and nodded when the 'sufficient balance' light turned green. "I'll need your voice approval," he said, gesturing at the amount that now appeared as a holographic projection above the mini-register.

"I approve seventy-five creds for one week's passage," Georgia said, deciding to err on the side of caution.

Larry gave her an appraising look as he returned her programmable cred. "Maybe you aren't as much of a

21

newbie as I took you for," he said. "Remind me to add you to the Stryx controller once we're underway. When do you want to leave?"

"Tomorrow. I'll go buy my supplies at the chandlery now, but I have to stop back at the paper's office in the morning to see about my advance. Is there anything I need to bring other than food and water?"

"Coffee or tea, if you're a caffeine freak like all of the reporters I've met. We don't brew in Zero-G, so buy the boxes with the built-in heater tabs. They aren't expensive. And bring at least two sets of workout clothes. I have a sterilizer unit that will keep clothes from stinking, but they feel kind of gross after getting soaked with sweat and drying out a few times."

"How long will we be spending in Zero-G between stops? I thought it was usually just a half a day or so."

"That's true between Stryx stations in the area, but some worlds and orbitals on the tunnel network are days away from the nearest entrance or exit, and that assumes we aren't going to any outer planets or moons in those systems. And tunnel traffic controllers intentionally stretch the time it takes to travel long distances to keep us from getting nutty. Our brains have trouble readjusting to large moves relative to the galactic core."

"I didn't know that," Georgia admitted in dismay. "What if weightlessness makes me sick? Can I buy medication?"

"You can, but I advise against it," Larry told her. "Drugs are fine for a few hours here and there, but we're going to be spending a lot of time in Zero-G, so you may as well tough it out and get acclimated. I know some tricks that will help you adjust."

Her new roommate, or captain, Georgia wasn't sure yet how to classify him, led her to the chandlery, and they arranged to leave right after lunch the next day. The man working behind the counter was a few years older than her, and as soon as she described her intention, he began grabbing items off various shelves and making a pile of them.

"I'll throw in a spool of twine," Kevin told her when his initial flurry of activity wound down. "I'm sure that Larry has his own, but he'll appreciate the gesture."

"What will I do with twine?"

"You'll see when you're in Zero-G," he replied, and began enumerating the goods he'd piled up. "Magnetic cleats, a week's supply of coffee at two boxes a day, a two week supply of water at six boxes a day, one week's worth of mystery meals in squeeze tubes—you're sure you don't want to choose?"

"I'm a food writer. I eat weird stuff for a living."

"Right. Well, I basically gave you one of everything I stock. A small sack of potatoes—"

"Are you sure I'll need those?" she interrupted.

"Just in case the squeeze tubes don't work out. Sharf two-man traders have a built-in microwave, and potatoes are foolproof and ideal for Zero-G cooking."

"What else do people eat?"

"Foods that stick to a spoon, at least if you don't move too fast. Baked beans in heavy sauce are popular, and some traders will eat anything from a can and just be careful about cleaning up after themselves. I gave you a half-dozen apples instead of the oranges you asked for. I don't stock citrus because it's surprisingly messy under weightless conditions."

"How about orange juice?"

"Squeeze tubes or boxes?"

"Which is cheaper?"

"Tubes."

"I'll take seven. What's in that yellow tube you already gave me?"

"Zero-G soap. Larry has a Dollnick shower installed."

"I can't use regular soap?"

"Gums up the filters. Your subtotal comes to forty-two creds and seventy centees. See anything else you want?"

"That's less than I thought it would be. How about something I can share with my, uh…"

"Captain," the chandler supplied the correct term. "Desserts and salty snacks are always popular, or if you want something that will last a long time, I just got in a shipment of rum-soaked fruitcakes."

"Like the ones people send around at Christmas?"

"Exactly."

"I think I'll go with pretzels."

Three

"Roland?" Walter addressed the chief editor of the free-lance department, who looked up from his desk to see the paper's managing editor accompanied by the publisher, Chastity Papamarkakis. "Do you have a minute?"

"For my boss and the owner? Always." Roland made a swiping motion over his display desk to dismiss his current work into storage and stood so that he wouldn't be the only one seated. "Is something wrong?"

"Have you been watching the Grenouthian news?" Chastity asked.

"I try to keep it to a minimum."

"Put it on and select their top story today."

Roland made a different gesture above his display desk, then selected an icon from the resulting hologram and dragged it to the right. A new holographic projection appeared, featuring a fair-haired teen dressed like the girl on the box lid of a popular brand of imported Swiss chocolates. She had a small microphone clipped to her collar and a press ID suspended on a lanyard around her neck.

"I'm Lena, for the Children's News Network, here with Matteo Allaman, president of the Combined Insurers Group," the girl began. "Matteo, I'm sure you already know what my first question will be, but for our viewers, can you explain what's so special about the Swiss government bond that came due today?"

"Certainly, Lena," the president said. "This unique hundred-year bond was issued shortly before the Stryx opened Earth and was the first of its kind to pay a negative nominal interest rate. Our company invested ten million francs in the issue for long-term planning."

"But why would anybody ever purchase a bond that pays a negative interest rate? I suppose it's not surprising that it was the only one of its kind."

"Perhaps I need to clarify my statement," Matteo said. "Government bonds with negative yields actually made up the majority of issuance at the time the Stryx opened Earth. The unique thing about this bond is that it was issued with a negative coupon, requiring purchasers to make regular interest payments to the Swiss treasury. At that time in Earth's history, national governments were issuing new debt on a daily basis, but most of the maturities ran from two years to thirty years, with the ten-year bond serving as the benchmark. Switzerland enjoyed one of the few governments ever deemed creditworthy enough to issue a hundred-year bond."

"Which guaranteed a loss for the purchaser," Lena observed.

"The bond's real value might have appreciated if Switzerland had experienced an extended period of deflation," Matteo pointed out. "It's true that investors with access to a vault would have done better to simply keep their savings in cash, but our money managers at the time had no way of knowing if interest rates would become even more negative in the future."

"So you're saying that your insurance company wanted to lock in a small loss for one hundred years rather than waiting and perhaps having the opportunity to lock in a bigger loss at a later date?"

"I wouldn't have put it exactly like that," the executive protested mildly. "You have to understand that our investment activity at all times is based on the prevailing economic theories."

"There was an economic theory that said paying a government to borrow your money was a good idea?"

"Actually, the whole concept of negative interest rates and coupons was supposed to be impossible. If our predecessors had been paying closer attention, they might have detected the problem in the early 21st century, when over a quarter of the world's government debt was already yielding real negative returns."

"You would think so," Lena said. "But you're using a lot of financial terms that may be difficult for our viewership to understand, so perhaps you could give an example?"

"Certainly. The particular issuance we purchased, in addition to carrying a negative coupon rate of 0.1%, sold at auction to institutional buyers at a premium of almost two percent, due to high demand."

"A premium is the opposite of a discount, meaning you paid more than the face value?"

"Exactly. I have the numbers right here. We paid just under one hundred and two francs per one hundred francs of face value for our ten-million-franc bond. For the last hundred years, we have been submitting annual payments to the Swiss treasury of ten thousand francs, the coupon interest we owed them for borrowing our money."

"So if I'm doing that math correctly, first you paid almost two hundred thousand francs for the privilege of loaning the Swiss government your ten million, and since that time, you've paid out another million francs because

27

of the negative coupon rate. Your original ten million franc investment has lost twelve percent of its value, not counting inflation."

"Very good," Matteo praised the teenage reporter. "If you're interested in a job when you finish school, please come and see me. But keep in mind that had there been deflation, we might have come out ahead."

"But there wasn't deflation."

"No, rather the opposite, I'm afraid, though nobody could have predicted the Stryx opening Earth and bringing us onto their tunnel network. Still, I like to think the fact that the one-hundred-year issue was oversubscribed says a great deal about the creditworthiness of the Swiss government. We can also boast being one of the few nations on Earth that remained fully independent and retained more than half of our pre-Opening population."

"That is much better than the international average," the girl agreed. "Technical language aside, can you tell our viewers why supposedly sophisticated investors were so eager to buy debt that paid negative interest rates back before the Stryx opened Earth?"

"I've made a study of the period and the answer is surprisingly simple," Matteo said. "The prevailing economic theories of the time all made the fatal assumption that investors are rational actors who think through the consequences of their decisions. In reality, investors just follow the herd."

The teen nodded her head in agreement, and then said, "This is Lena, reporting for the Children's News Network in Zurich. Over to you in Paris, Samantha."

Instead of Samantha in Paris, a furry alien resembling a giant bunny appeared, and he seemed to be having trouble breathing. The Grenouthian news presenter struggled mightily to compose himself, but his lips were still trembling with suppressed mirth when he began to speak.

"And there you have it, straight from the Human's mouth," the presenter said. "Negative coupon rates on government bonds, Earth's contribution to financial engineering. Turning to news from more serious species, in Verlock—"

Roland waved the hologram out of existence and turned back to Walter and Chastity.

"We've already contacted CNN for the print rights to Lena's interview," Walter said. "Those kids have a nose for stories like that."

"I'm sure you know that we negotiated deals with the Earth's surviving news syndicates not long after I started the Galactic Free Press," Chastity told Roland. "Unfortunately, most of the papers supporting those syndicates have since gone bankrupt."

"If you're about to say that you're opening an Earth bureau and you want me to be the head, I'd rather stay on Union Station and take a pay cut to work for EarthCent Intelligence," Roland told them. "It's not that I don't appreciate all you've done for me, but I have a thing about Earth."

"Don't worry," Walter said. "For the time being, we're focused on expanding our relationship with the Children's News Network and the student newspapers. But you know that the maximum age of their reporters is eighteen, so using them as investigative journalists is out of the question."

"I see," Roland said. "Is this about the young woman who came in yesterday?"

"Who was that?" Chastity asked.

"Georgia Hunt. She grew up on Earth, even went through the New University system there, and she just made the move to freelance because she wants to do investigative journalism."

"Our local food writer? But I count on her for reviews of all the new restaurants that open here. They come and go so fast."

"I agreed to buy any food stories she sends in while she's pursuing her big story," Roland said. "Georgia told me she was leaving Union Station right after lunch, so I'm afraid we're too late if you wanted to offer her an Earth assignment."

"I think she'll need a little seasoning first," Walter punned, drawing a groan from both the publisher and the freelance editor.

"We've put together a list of the journalists from Earth whose stories we ran over the years," Chastity continued. "If you have a freelancer with business sense headed that direction, we'll pay a bonus for contacting the names on the list to see if they're interested in forming a group to work with us. I'd rather subsidize a new independent syndicate until they can get on their feet than open a permanent office of our own on Earth."

"Got anybody in mind for the job?" Walter asked the freelance editor.

"How about Ellen?" Roland suggested. "She came up through the student newspapers while her parents were working on a Dollnick ag world, and she's been freelancing for us the last ten years to supplement her trading income."

"She wrote the series of articles we ran last year about longevity treatment scams," Chastity recalled.

"That's her. She's tough as they come, and she would have won our investigative journalist of the year award if Andreas hadn't uncovered that price-fixing scandal involving mercenary contractors."

"Isn't she the one who got blitzed at the awards dinner and fell off the stage?" Walter asked.

"Ellen has a bit of a control problem with social drinking, but it's never interfered with her work."

"Has she ever been to Earth?"

"That I'm not sure, but I'll get ahold of her and let you know if she's available."

"Works for me," Chastity said. "Walter?"

"I suppose it's worth a shot," the managing editor said. "Roland, let me know if you need more resources. The two of us have to run if we're going to make the Grenouthian reception."

"Why do you go when you know they're only going to gloat about scooping us on the Swiss bond story?"

"Because if you let them brag a little, they always end up giving away something they're still working on," Chastity said. "Besides, they did beat us fair and square."

As soon as his employers left, Roland pulled up the database he used to track the location of all the freelance journalists who were regular contributors. He scrolled through the list with impatient hand gestures until he located the reporter he was looking for and barked a short laugh.

"Libby," Roland said out loud. "Could you ping Ellen for me?"

"I'm afraid she's muted her implant."

"Can you tell me her exact location?"

"I don't think that would be appropriate at the moment."

"How about where she isn't? Could you tell me if she's sleeping it off on her ship?"

"She is not."

"Is she on a date?"

"I wouldn't call it that."

"In a bar?" Roland waited a moment to confirm that Libby wasn't responding, and rose from his desk. "One of those dives near the Empire Convention Center?"

"Does she ever drink anywhere else?"

"You don't approve," Roland continued the conversation over his implant as he threaded his way through the newsroom. "Ellen claims she gets all of her best leads in bars."

"There are better ways to meet people. I offered her a discounted membership to my dating service."

"I don't think she's the type."

"You have an incoming ping from Katya Wysecki."

"I'll take it," Roland said, stepping into the lift tube capsule and instructing it, "Empire Convention Center," before continuing, "Hello, Katya."

"Have you found me a replacement for Georgia?" a woman's voice came over his implant.

"How is that my job? Besides, she's going to be submitting food articles during her travels, and now they'll come out of my budget instead of yours. I'd say you won on the exchange."

"You don't have anybody who wants to move from freelance to full-time?"

"I don't understand. I would have thought with all the publicity around the All Species Cookbook launch you'd be flooded with candidates."

"The problem is that none of them can write. I wasted the entire day reading story samples from would-be reporters that were no more than recipes. Food writing requires a certain flair."

"How about Scotch Frank? He recently moved back to Union Station and he's looking to pick up more work."

"Your distillery reporter?"

"He doesn't just cover distilleries. A lot of the micro-breweries he visited were combined with pubs, and I remember you telling me how much you enjoyed his piece about wine tasters."

"That was hilarious. Okay, have him ping me, and if it works out, I'll put him on our payroll to make up for you taking on Georgia."

"You still win because they'll both be writing about food. Hello?"

"She disconnected," the Stryx librarian informed him.

The doors slid open and Roland immediately turned left in the corridor, heading away from the convention center towards the strip of bars that culminated in the station's red-light district.

"Libby," he subvoced. "Have you ever played Hot/Cold?"

"You're really pushing it today," the station librarian replied. "I wouldn't be doing this if you weren't on Ellen's emergency contact list. You're getting warmer... warmer... warmer... colder."

Roland turned around and headed back towards the last bar he had passed, a seedy-looking place without a name above the doors.

"Warmer... hot," Libby declared over the freelance editor's implant as he entered. "You're on your own."

Roland strained his eyes in the dim lighting trying to locate his wayward freelancer. There was a long bar running the length of one side of the room, and the other side featured a row of high-backed booths, obviously intended for privacy. Looking closer at the table in one of the empty booths, he saw a small machine that he initially took for an antique jukebox remote, but on closer inspection proved to offer a Dollnick audio suppression field for one cred per hour. Then loud laughter from the end of the bar caught his attention.

"You almost made me soil my armor," a man's voice protested. "I've got to hit the head."

"Hit it for me too," a woman's voice replied.

"Ellen," Roland called out as he approached the reporter. "Fancy bumping into you here."

"I'm not available," she replied immediately. "I'm leaving tomorrow and I can't tell you where I'm going because it's a sheecrit."

"Did you mean secret?"

"That's what I said. Are you getting something to drink? Frode. Give my editor a drink."

"No, thank you," Roland said, waving off the Drazen bartender. "This is a major opportunity, Ellen. I wouldn't have tracked you down otherwise. Our publisher and managing editor are—"

"Can I get some peanuts?" the reporter interrupted him, grabbing at the Drazen's sleeve as he passed. "The good ones, with the salt."

"Try to concentrate for just a minute, Ellen. There's an opportunity on Earth—"

"How did you know I was going to Earth?" the reporter demanded. "Did you sic EarthCent Intelligence on me?"

"I didn't know you were going to Earth, but it's highly fortuitous. The old news syndicates have broken down and we're left dependent on the student-run papers and Children's News Network—"

"Reporting for the student papers was the best job I ever had, even though it didn't pay," Ellen interrupted again. "Hey, what happened to Jordan?" she asked the bartender as he placed a small dish of peanuts in front of her.

"He snuck past behind you when he came out of the bathroom," the Drazen replied. "It's just as well. His wife usually comes looking for him around now."

"I have a list of the Earth-based investigative journalists who we've published in the past, and we want you to contact them and offer our help in setting up their own news syndicate," Roland continued unperturbed. "We don't expect it to happen all at once, so if you take the job, it means a bonus and regular stops at Earth, which could be quite profitable for you."

"What's the bonus?"

"We didn't discuss an exact figure, but—"

"I need fifteen hundred creds."

"That much!?"

"I'm working on the scoop of the century but the expenses are killing me."

"So you're asking me to join you in a suicide pact?" Roland stole a few peanuts from the reporter before she could move the dish out of his reach. "All right. I'll get you fifteen hundred, but I expect you to spend a full month on Earth so that you'll be reachable by the people you contact. After that, we'll talk."

"You're a prince, boss. As long as I can leave in time for Rendezvous. Are you sure you don't want a drink?"

"How about I take you for something to eat instead? My wife is with the kids at a bowling party and they're getting pizza."

"What's the damage, Frode?" Ellen called to the Drazen.

35

"Jordan was running a tab on his programmable cred—I took it out of that."

"That's why you're my favorite bartender on Union Station," the reporter said, and slapped down a two-cred coin as a tip. "Where are we eating, boss?"

"How about the food court at the Empire Convention Center?"

"Sure, that's close." Ellen staggered against the editor when she slipped off her barstool and began thumping her right thigh with her fist. "Went to sleep on me. I must have been sitting here longer than I realized."

"So how's life treating you outside of work?" Roland asked, staying close to her side in case she lost her balance again.

"It's been a tough year for independent traders and I've seen too many bankruptcy auctions. I'm really looking forward to Rendezvous this year because the new council we elect will decide whether or not the Traders Guild will join the Conference of Sovereign Human Communities."

"I caught a Rendezvous many years ago and you traders have a funny way of electioneering."

"But we do vote. And you'd think everybody would be in favor of joining, but some of the old-school traders are classic loners. Most of the young traders, well, you can wait to find out until I submit my story."

"This Earth assignment could turn into a full-time gig if it works out."

"You mean sell my ship and settle down on a big ball of rock? Not a chance. I may not have been born a trader like some of them, but it's in my blood."

"Then your blood must be getting crowded because there's a heck of an investigative journalist in there too, at least when she's not swimming in alcohol."

Four

"If you won't go back, just kill me and get it over with," Georgia groaned.

"We can't turn around in the tunnel, and we're already halfway there," Larry lied to soften the blow.

"Really? You're not just saying that?"

"Do you realize you haven't thrown up in almost three hours?" he asked in reply.

"That's because there's nothing left in my stomach. Would you please stop moving?"

"I'm not moving. Space sickness happens because the data from your inner ear doesn't match what you see and your brain goes whacky trying to adjust."

"Are you saying there's something wrong with my implant?"

"No, it's the old-school mammal stuff. Did you get a good night's sleep?"

"I was up most of last night tying up loose ends before we left. I guess I should have planned further ahead."

"Sleep deprivation makes Zero-G sickness worse. I should have warned you," Larry said sympathetically.

"You said you knew some tricks that would help me through it," Georgia reminded him in an accusatory tone.

"I'm saving those tricks for later because you're not that bad. I had a passenger once who lost control of his bowels and—"

"Not helping," she interrupted. "How long is it going to last?"

"I think you're already coming out of it," he lied again.

"If there was just something to see out of the porthole instead of the tunnel void. I used to get motion sick traveling in floater buses back on Earth, but if I could sit in the front and look forward, it was better."

"Space sickness is the opposite of terrestrial motion sickness," Larry explained. "That's why I keep telling you to close your eyes, or at least focus on something small. You should try reading on your tab."

"Are you sure? That's the last thing I would do on a bus."

"Trust me. Besides, if you were really that sick, you wouldn't be able to ask so many questions."

"Comes with the profession." Closing her eyes once again, Georgia found that this time it provided almost immediate relief. "Keep talking."

"About what?"

"I don't know. Tell me about yourself. I still can't believe I'm going to be living in one room with a complete stranger."

"Come on, I'm sure you checked me out with your paper. I'll bet you reporters all have free access to the EarthCent Intelligence business database."

"I might have asked them to run a criminal background check, but how much does that really tell you about a person?" she asked rhetorically. "Only that he hasn't been caught yet. The truth is, I was so desperate to get started on my new career that I would have come even if you were a notorious axe murderer. Oh, and the report from EarthCent Intelligence said that your credit is good."

"That's the most important thing in my world. Anybody can get into a drunken bar brawl on some alien station and end up with a criminal record, but good credit has to be earned."

"Is that how you got your nose broken? In a bar brawl?"

"No comment," Larry said, self-consciously touching his imperfectly healed nose.

"Are you married?"

"Do I look married? No, don't open your eyes." He paused a moment, considering his answer. "I was married. It didn't work out. I don't want to talk about it."

"Okay," Georgia said cautiously. "Family?"

"I'm from a trader family. My parents still live on their ship, and I have a brother who was a trader until he married some grounder he met on a Verlock open world and went native. My uncle, dad's brother, is a trader too, and I have a couple of cousins who work a two-man ship together. My grandparents settled on Void station when my grandmother had enough of living a quarter of her life in Zero-G, but my grandfather still owns a ship, and he takes consignment deliveries to keep a hand in. How about you?"

"My parents are crazy," Georgia said bluntly. "My father insisted that everything that ever went wrong in his life was the fault of an alien conspiracy, and my mother won't even accept that the Stryx exist. I grew up in a sort of a commune of squatters on an abandoned college campus, and nobody talked about the outside world because it would always end in an argument."

"So how does your mom explain the tunnel network?"

"She doesn't, and even though you could see the space elevator from our kitchen window on a clear day, she pretended it wasn't there."

"How about the moon landing?"

"Nope, but at least I can understand her on that one. It is kind of hard to believe that people made it to the moon all those years ago without alien help."

"Our scientists used to be pretty handy with rockets, probably because they made good weapons, but they're next to useless for commercial space travel due to the fuel-to-weight ratio," Larry said. "Do you mind if I hop on the stationary bike while we talk? I'm used to exercising at least six hours a day in Zero-G and I feel like I'm being lazy just floating here."

"You're going to ride the bike upside-down?"

"I told you, there is no such thing in space. Tell me when you feel ready to try one of the machines and I'll help you get hooked up. And if you think you're done with that sick-up bag, I'll put it in the trash."

"Take it," Georgia said, relinquishing her death grip on the sealable pouch that contained the barely-digested remnants of her lunch. "Why did you insist that we eat before leaving when you knew there was a good chance I'd be sick?"

"Having something to throw up beats the dry heaves." He double-checked that the bag was properly sealed, and then gently shoved off the back of her chair to propel himself to the locker set aside for the trash. There he placed the sick-bag into a larger garbage sack and used a short piece of elastic to tie it shut. After putting the garbage back in the locker, he pushed off for the exercise bike.

"I thought spaceships all had disposal chutes," Georgia commented.

"You were watching? You must really be feeling better then. And bigger space ships do have disposal chutes but they don't dump into space. On Stryx stations and alien orbitals, everything is either recycled or atomized, which is also a form of recycling because the atoms can be used for something. Traders don't have a lot of waste, mainly food packaging, and we have to pay to get rid of it when we're docked or parked."

"I always assumed the trash got dumped in space."

"Aliens have fought wars over littering, it's nothing we can afford to fool around with," Larry told her. He slipped his feet through the pedal straps and fastened the waist harness to keep his butt on the seat. "Besides, it wouldn't work in the tunnel. The way it's been explained to me, even if I cycled the trash out through the airlock it would travel right along with us. Then we'd get in trouble with traffic control at the other end."

"Traffic control? I thought the tunnels were just open."

"Seriously? It's a toll system, though it all works through the Stryx-supplied ship controllers so it's not like we have to stop and pay. Earth is just a probationary tunnel network member so we get the option to go shares rather than paying a flat rate. All of the traders I know work that way."

"So you're in business with the Stryx?" Georgia asked, carefully tilting her head back until she could see where Larry was pedaling away like he was climbing a hill in first gear.

"Nothing so grand. I use the mini-register to keep track of my business, cash is on the honor system, and the Stryx traffic controllers access that information and debit their percentage when I enter a tunnel."

"You really are upside-down, you know."

"If you're well enough to watch me pedaling, you should try to drink some water. Once you're rehydrated, a little exercise will make you feel even better."

"Can you help me get to my food locker?"

"Try it yourself and I'll come to the rescue if you get stranded. Moving around in weightlessness is easier than it looks, almost too easy. The trick is not to push off anything too hard because you have to be able to stop yourself without bouncing when you get there."

"Is that what all the ropes are for? I thought they were pull cords for some kind of emergency system."

"I went with safety lines running through rings welded to the bulkhead because that's how I grew up. Some traders wear magnetic gloves so they can stick anywhere in a steel ship, and of course, everybody has magnetic cleats for their boots. I only use those on board when I work in the cargo hold."

"The chandler sold me a pair but I put them away with my food. You know what? I think I'm hungry."

"Start with the water," Larry advised her. "Actually, start with removing your safety restraints or you aren't going anywhere."

"Right." Georgia unbuckled the four-point harness that kept her strapped into the padded acceleration chair and then took a deep breath. "Here I go." A few seconds later, she slammed into the lockers but managed to grab one of the safety lines to keep from drifting off.

"So what did you do wrong?" Larry asked in a calm voice.

"Why did I hit so hard? I barely pushed off at all."

"You started with your knees bent and then you extended until your legs were straight. It doesn't feel like a lot of work because you're weightless, but your mass is the same as it would be on Earth or Union Station. Next time, try pushing off with just your toes. Good job taking the force on your arms, though. For a second there I was worried you were going to hit your head."

"I'm not uncoordinated, I was just surprised." Georgia opened her food locker and got out a box of Union Station Springs water. "Do you want one?"

"I'm set with recycled supply, and just so you know, it's considered rude to offer water from your own stock in trader circles. It means you think that the person you're with is too incompetent to plan for their own survival."

"Sounds like you have a lot of rules. How does this work?"

"Pull the straw off the side, jab it through the seal, and then you can suck the water out. We only had squeeze tubes when I was a kid, but the boxes are better because you'd really have to work at it to cause an accident."

"Nothing is coming out," she reported after some fruit-less sucking.

"Make sure your hand isn't covering the vent holes on the bottom. If the air can't get in to fill the space between the box and the bladder, it's like trying to create a vacu-um." He pedaled on in silence for almost a minute before asking, "Is it alright now?"

"Finished," Georgia declared, and crushed the empty box for emphasis. "I'll put it in the garbage."

"That goes into recycling, the yellow bag. I keep it in the same locker as the garbage bag because we don't generate much of either."

"How can you tell what's recycling and what's gar-bage?"

"Okay, I called it garbage because I don't know how squeamish you are, but the real deal is that the blue bag is biological waste and the yellow bag is everything else."

"You have a whole bag dedicated to vomit?"

"Maybe we should save this discussion for after you've eaten," Larry suggested.

"I'm all better now, really, and I'm the least squeamish person I know. Just tell me."

"If you're sure," he said, clicking the tension setting on the exercise bike up a notch and dropping his pedaling speed. "Have you ever used a Zero-G toilet?"

"No, but what does that have to do with it?"

"Like I said, we can't dump anything in space. On a small ship like this, the waste reprocessing system is limited to recovering the water, which is relatively easy. The stuff that's left over, the solids, get baked into briquettes by the toilet and vacuum-sealed in disposable pouches. I empty them into the biological waste bag every few days to keep the receptacle from overfilling."

"So when you said you're set with recycled water, you mean that you drink…"

"We're in space, Georgia. Everybody drinks recycled wastewater, the only question is whether it's distilled with minerals added, like what I get back from the toilet, or whether it's gone through some kind of natural filtration process, like the water you bought on Union Station. I'm sure the only reason the chandler sold you so many water boxes was because you told him it was your first time on a small ship. We've all heard stories about Earthers getting dehydrated because they refuse to drink recycled water. That and it doesn't hurt to have a backup supply in case something goes wrong."

"I thought you said we'd drink the shower water if something went wrong."

"I said some traders have resorted to that, but only if the toilet recycling system fails and they don't have any other supply." He increased the tension setting again and his breath began to come harder. "Not sleepy yet?"

"Should I be? I'm really kind of hungry. Do you want to eat?"

"You go ahead. I'm going to get in at least two more hours of exercise first. I showed you the small microwave if you need to heat something up, but that's the only kitchen equipment we can use in Zero-G."

"Hey, I'm stuck!"

Larry craned his neck around to look at his passenger and chuckled. "You're not stuck, you're unstuck. You must have let go of the rope while you were drinking and accidentally pushed off just enough to drift out of reach of the safety line."

"What should I do? I read somewhere if you're adrift in space you can move by throwing something. I could throw my empty water box."

"It doesn't have enough mass and I'd rather you didn't start throwing things on the bridge. I'll get the bot to rescue you," he concluded, and called, "Genie?"

"Who? What bot?"

"Genie, my cargo bot. She's in her charging bay in the hold so it will take a minute for her to get here. I paid for an upgrade to my ship controller so Genie responds to voice instructions."

"And the controller is artificial intelligence?"

"Controllers aren't sentient, but in addition to doing all of the navigation and providing limited Stryxnet access, they're programmed to handle most of the situations that come up in space. Which reminds me, I have to add you as a guest."

"What will that do?"

"If I had a heart attack right now or got knocked unconscious, the controller won't respond to your voice since I haven't added you yet. If I didn't recover, we'd eventually end up returning to my home port, which is registered as Union Station."

"How eventually?"

"The default no-response timeout is seventy-two hours," Larry said. "Once you're added as a guest, if I'm disabled, you could tell it to return us home immediately. I didn't pay for the medbay option so the controller has limited ability to scan our health status, but if it determined I was in really bad condition, it would let you specify any Stryx station. That and answer your questions rather than ignoring you."

"So how do we do this?"

"Controller. Recognize Georgia Hunt as an official guest."

"Georgia Hunt added to manifest," a female voice responded. "Please repeat the following sentence for voice registration—My name is Georgia Hunt."

"My name is Georgia Hunt," the reporter repeated dutifully.

"Recognition complete."

"Is that it? Are there any instructions?"

"It's a natural language interface and it's always listening. You can address the controller directly, or like with Genie, it can usually figure out that you're talking to it through context. Where is that bot?"

"Genie was in deep charge mode and has just completed self-test," the controller replied.

"I never actually heard of people owning bots. I thought they were an advanced species thing," Georgia said.

"People have been building robots for centuries, though Genie was manufactured by the Sharf as an add-on accessory for this type of ship. Don't be disappointed when you see her. She's basically just a box with mechanical arms for cargo manipulation, but she's pretty strong." There was a loud buzz, and Larry explained, "That's the alarm for when the hatch between the bridge and the cargo hold opens. I usually leave it open all the time once we're underway, but it's good practice to close it during arrivals and departures because that's when most accidents happen."

"Here she comes," Georgia said, watching as the bot emerged from the hatch. "Good, Genie. Come here and rescue me."

"She's not a dog," Larry said, but to their mutual surprise, the bot navigated directly to the reporter and closed a pincer around one of her wrists. "Don't worry, Genie won't hurt you."

"I wasn't worried, but how can I make her take me back to the garbage locker?"

"See how the ship controller is able to parse your meaning?" Larry said, as the bot gently propelled Georgia towards the safety line that ran between the lockers.

"You're sure it's not artificial intelligence?"

"I've been living on board for eight years and I would have noticed. And why would an AI agree to stay on a little tin can like this? They have better things to do."

"Well, I'm going to thank her anyway. Thank you, Genie."

"You're welcome," the ship's controller replied.

"You can return to your charging bay, Genie," Larry said.

As the bot floated off towards the hatch, Georgia put her empty water box in the recycling bag, this time being careful to hook the safety line with her elbow to keep her hands free, and then she opened her food locker again and began rummaging through the squeeze tubes.

"Hey, they won't stay put!"

"Actually, stuff remains exactly where you place it in Zero-G, but only if you're not moving yourself when you let it go. Kids who grow up on small spaceships can do it without thinking, but people who experience weightlessness for the first time as an adult may never get the hang of it."

"This is too much work, I'm just going to pick one at random," Georgia said. She proceeded to do just that, and then quickly closed the locker before the rest of her food could drift off. "Chicken cacciatore with rice?" she read off the label.

"Chicken in tomato sauce with bell pepper and onion," Larry told her. "I thought you said you were a food writer."

"I know what chicken cacciatore is, I just never expected to be eating it out of a squeeze tube. Do you know if they use real chicken, or is it vegetable protein."

"Kind of late to be asking that if you're a vegetarian, but I think the brand stocked in the chandlery uses vat-grown meat."

"I'm not a vegetarian, I just wondered because the chandler didn't say anything about refrigeration."

"It's all irradiated, lasts for years without spoiling. So here's the thing," Larry continued, easing off the pedals and twisting to watch her. "You can warm it in the micro-

48

wave, but if you overdo it the tube will burst and we'll have a real mess to clean up. They make the squeeze tubes with a little steam release valve so you can heat them within reason before the contents get pressurized, but do me a favor and be really careful since it's your first time."

"I'll set it for five seconds and keep checking it," Georgia said, stretching for the next safety line, and then pulling herself in front of the microwave. "Where's the keypad?"

"I can operate the microwave for you," the ship's controller announced. "Will five seconds on 'warm' be sufficient?"

"Yes, thank you," the reporter said, placing the transparent squeeze tube, which was about the size of a burrito, into the small microwave. "Ready when you are."

The light in the microwave turned on, it hummed for five seconds, and the light blinked off and the ship's controller announced, "Ding."

"I taught it that," Larry said from halfway between the exercise bike and the rock climbing machine to which he was transferring.

"Not even lukewarm," Georgia complained, and returned the tube to the microwave. "Can we do that again, Controller?" Three iterations later, she turned her head towards Larry and asked, "How long is this going to take?"

"I usually go for ninety seconds. The red mouthpiece will pop up when it's done."

"Why didn't you tell me?"

"It's better to learn this stuff on your own, at least, that's the way my parents taught me."

"Could I get, uh, seventy seconds, Controller?" Georgia requested. A little over a minute later, there was a ding, and she had a hot, but not too hot, tube of chicken caccia-tore with rice in her hand. After a brief inspection, she asked, "How do I break the seal in the mouthpiece?"

"Just squeeze it gently between your thumb and fore-finger on the flats until you feel it give. The mouthpiece is actually semi-rigid, and the seal is a hard plastic disc that's been scribed to break easily. The halves remain attached, so if you don't finish off the tube, you can push them closed and then stick a cork in the mouthpiece."

A few more minutes passed, and then Georgia said, "I can't believe how good this tastes. Are all of the squeeze tubes like this?"

"They aren't bad, but you kind of started with the best one. It's hard to beat chunks of anything in tomato sauce."

Five

"I hate Earth," Ellen complained, rubbing the sore spot on her head. "It's cold, it smells funny, and it just dropped something on me!"

"That something is why we're here," John reminded her, "and if you let your hair grow out again, the acorn wouldn't have hurt half as much."

"How many male traders do you know with long hair?" she countered. "It's a pain in the butt in Zero-G. Getting a buzz cut at the festival on Dorf Seven is the smartest thing I've done in years."

"No, the smartest thing you've done in years was agreeing to meet me here. I know, I know," he added before she could respond. "I owed you for stealing your blanket perch at the Corner Station gadget festival, but I did get there first."

Ellen bent to pick up the acorn that she was sure had left a dent in her skull and examined it carefully. "Are you sure there's a market for these things?"

"The Huktra are nuts about them," John said, and pulled a face when she didn't react. "I ran into one of their traders who visited Earth on a culinary tour package deal and he happened to pick a bunch of acorns off the ground. Myort said they were better than anything he ate in any of the restaurants."

"Why isn't he here now if he thinks acorns are so great, or better yet, why isn't he setting up an export business?"

"Because Myort hated Earth even more than you do. The rain turned his scales blue and people kept screaming and running away when they saw him."

"Earthers are afraid of blue scales?"

"They're afraid of quarter-ton aliens who look like hungry dragons. Besides, Myort didn't know that acorns were good to eat until he got back home and found a few left in a side pocket of his luggage. I guess he originally picked them up to have something to throw at people who pointed at him, and it was pure chance I ran into him before he ate the last one."

"That sounds more like the Huktras I know," Ellen acknowledged. She waved her hand to indicate the expansive, badly overgrown town green where they had both landed their trade ships. "So who owns all of this?"

"My parents claim to have been the last residents to pay taxes, but since my mother was the town treasurer and my father was the mayor, they were just transferring money between pockets. This whole area was losing population even before the Stryx opened Earth, and after that, it was like a dam broke. By the time my parents boarded up the house and left for a Dollnick ag world as contract workers, pretty much the whole county was abandoned."

"So who tends the acorn trees?" Ellen asked, dropping her shoulder bag to the ground and accepting a rake from John.

"They're oaks, and they take care of themselves. Listen, the only reason I brought you in on this is because I know it's a one-time deal and I owed you a favor. By the time we finish selling our cargos, word will spread across the tunnel network, and one of the big export businesses here will start harvesting acorns. They'll drive the price down to where you and I couldn't afford to compete."

"So you're saying that if you thought you could keep it secret and get rich by yourself, you would?"

"Of course, and you would too. I don't see you traveling with a partner."

"You know why that is," Ellen replied, giving him a look. "So where's your rake?"

"I've got this shoulder thing from my mercenary stint," John said, moving his right arm through an abbreviated throwing motion and faking a pained grimace. "I figure that you can rake and I can shovel. We'll fill the sacks in no time."

"And you'll load them into my cargo hold first."

"I'll alternate," he countered.

Ellen made a 'ptew' sound as if she were spitting on her palm and offered her hand to shake. "Deal," they both declared solemnly, and then she set to work raking acorns off the old asphalt.

A small herd of deer moved about in the high grass not a stone's throw away, working on their own harvest. Occasionally, the oldest doe would stop feeding and eye the humans, though it was unclear if she was checking to make sure they maintained their distance, or simply annoyed by the intrusion.

"Break time," John declared after two solid hours of shoveling acorns into the lightweight Frunge cargo sacks that could hold anything from grain to ball bearings without ever ripping or even becoming discolored. "I've only been filling your bags half as full as mine so you'll be able to lift them without help."

"Maybe I'll find a buyer in Zero-G," Ellen said, sitting down on a sunken granite curbstone and stretching out her legs. After a sip from her canteen, she asked, "I wonder if there's anywhere around here to get some fresh water, just for a change?"

"Even if the pipes hadn't frozen and burst by now, the pumps haven't been on since my parents left, and there wouldn't be any power to run them in any case."

"I thought little towns on Earth had wells and you could just haul the water up in buckets."

"In rural areas like this, it was a mix of wells and reservoirs, but the wells were deep boreholes with electric pumps at the bottom, and the reservoirs had filter systems that needed to be maintained. My father was only in his thirties when they pulled up stakes, but he told me a story about putting on climbing gear as a teenager and painting the water tower." John leaned on his shovel and pointed at a rusty metal tank mounted on a steel framework at the top of a rise behind the skeletal remains of some houses.

"It doesn't look like anybody's painted it in twenty-five years."

"Because that would have been fifty years ago. It's kind of surprising that it's still standing, but I guess now that those trees growing around it are getting big, either their roots will lift the concrete pad until it tips over, or one of them will fall on it."

"How come you know so much about Earth stuff?"

"I brought my dad back to visit a couple of times after I got my ship, and you know I read history books on my tab while I'm on the exercise equipment. What do you do with the time these days?"

"I watch alien dramas or work on my freelance stuff. I can't read while I'm exercising, and I've gotten to where audiobooks put me to sleep."

"You can fall asleep while you're working out?"

"Not sleep-sleep, but I kind of drift off, if you know what I mean," Ellen said. "Anybody who didn't know you would think you grew up on a trade ship. You just give out that kind of vibe."

"I guess I work at it," John admitted. "We're both in a business where it's important to get people to trust us. Speaking of work…"

"You're the one who called this break," Ellen reminded him, pulling her gloves back on and taking up the rake. "I'd just as soon keep going until it gets dark so we aren't here all week."

"It's not lion country if that's what you're worried about. That's the other side of the planet."

"How about the other two?" she asked, as John stretched a new sack over the collapsible holder.

"Other two what?"

"Tigers and bears. Aren't they the big three?"

"I wouldn't be surprised if the woods are crawling with bears but they're probably shy of people. If there was anything dangerous around, I think our neighbors there would tell us," he added, motioning towards the deer. "Another trader I know makes regular visits to rural locations on Earth to barter for cheese and smoked meats, and he says that the farmers are always complaining about wolves and coyotes."

"So this area isn't completely abandoned."

"It's a patchwork. Towns like this that were never more than a couple of churches and stores serving the local mill didn't have much reason to continue when the population dropped too far. You've never been to Earth?"

"Never had a reason."

They worked on in silence, saving their breath for the job. Ellen raked together huge piles of acorns and John

55

shoveled them into sacks and humped them back to one or the other of their holds. By the time they'd put a dent into the bumper crop on the remains of the old pavement, the sun was dropping below the horizon.

"Not a bad day's work," John said. "Your hold has plenty more room but I'm not sure about the weight. What are you carrying in the bins?"

"Don't remind me," Ellen groaned, flexing her tired shoulders. "I got talked into taking a consignment of ore to Borten Four—"

"Are you following me everywhere now?"

"You're going too? The ore needs to end up at the mining habitat that supports the asteroid belt operations. It's a favor for Big Kim, and I think he was doing it as a favor for somebody else. Those bins have seen the inside of more holds the last cycle than a crooked customs inspector."

"You're literally carrying rocks to a mining habitat?"

"Ore. I think it's all part of an elaborate prank and I can't help wondering if the joke is on me."

"It just seems like a lot of wear and tear on your fuel pack to land on Earth with that kind of mass when you're going to have to carry it back into space."

"How about you?"

"What?"

"Something came up with the paper and I'm going to be staying on Earth until Rendezvous. Want to take my ore to Borten Four? You'll be doing Big Kim a favor."

"I need a little more reason than that, Ellen."

"You can keep half of my acorns, but you have to make me dinner."

"Are you serious? Those sacks are worth real money."

"What I mean is you can take all of my acorns, but I'll settle for half of the money from them if the Huktras are

56

really buyers. At least I'm eliminating my risk if the trade is a bust."

"If they don't sell, I can always throw them at obnoxious people. My father said something about weevils, but hopefully by sticking to the acorns on what's left of the roads and parking lots we can reduce the number."

John carried the last sack back to his ship and Ellen accompanied him with the rake and the shovel.

"Hey, did ground control even contact you when we were coming in?" she asked. "I didn't hear a peep."

"I told tunnel traffic control where I was going when I exited. Didn't you get queried?"

"Yeah, but that's Stryx traffic control, not Earth. Or don't they even care here?"

"They're probably overworked. I'll bet hundreds of independent traders are landing in out-of-the-way places every day looking for antiques they can fob off on the aliens as stolen museum pieces."

"I hear about that all the time but I've never actually met a trader who makes a living at it."

John dumped the sack on top of the others and stretched a piece of cargo netting across the load out of habit, even though he had no intention of lifting off that night. "I think the traders with established customer lists for antiques tend not to talk about it because they don't want to invite competition. Did you hear about that crazy new scheme for sharing market data?"

"I signed up," Ellen said, watching him out of the corner of her eye. "I've already earned a nine-star trust rating."

"Sounds like you're working on a story, but I know better than to pry. Why don't you go clean up while I make us something? If you put out your camp gear, we can eat outside."

"If you're implying I stink, you stink twice as bad, so do us both a favor and take a shower while the grub is warming up."

A half an hour later, John emerged from his two-man Sharf trader carrying a large tray with both hands. Ellen had already set up folding chairs and a table between their ships and was sipping wine from a metal cup.

"You went all out," John observed, indicating the wine bottle. "I thought you preferred quantity over quality."

"I took two cases in trade for an industrial spool of copper wire," Ellen replied, ignoring the dig at her drinking habits.

"The standard spool? Doesn't sound like much of a deal on your part."

"The wine is surprisingly good, and I'd been trying to unload that wire ever since I took it in trade for a broken Frunge wing set."

"Where did you get the wings?" John asked, propping one edge of the tray on the folding table while unloading it with the other hand.

"Failed vacation," Ellen told him. "I signed the waiver to skip flying lessons because I was short on time and I ended up crashing before I got off the ground."

"How is that even possible?"

"You'd have to ask the guy who taxied into me. He waived the lessons too. Anyway, the Frunge rental place kept my deposit and I became the proud owner of a broken set of wings, though the actuator still has some life in it."

"I guess a broken wing set for a spool of copper isn't a bad deal."

"Plus I was tired of looking at those wings in my hold. Is that lasagna with meat sauce?"

"Yeah, but I think the meat sauce is fake. I've got a couple hundred packages of it left if you're interested in a bit of barter. This whole meal is freeze-dried, including the vegetables, and it lasts for years. It's all good stuff, but I get tired of eating it every day."

"What did you trade for it?"

"Did you hear about the Ark?"

"Sure, that was less than a year ago. The crazy cult leader who thought he could turn an old freighter into a colony ship and brought his followers along. It's a miracle they didn't all die."

"They came close," John said, setting the empty tray on the ground and taking his seat. "I was on my way to do some trading at Four Sisters, which was the hot mining play at the time. Would you believe there were almost three-hundred people, including babies and grandparents, all crammed into this ancient Horten freighter in Zero-G and puking their guts out all over each other? The cult had bought it as scrap in Earth orbit and they didn't even do a basic refit. The real miracle is that the drive got them to the tunnel entrance."

"What were they doing in the Four Sisters System?"

"Their leader had a vision that it was some kind of paradise. Can you imagine? They could easily have found a town in better shape than this one to take over right here on Earth and nobody would have said a thing about it. Instead, they begged, borrowed, or stole enough money for a flying piece of junk and headed for an asteroid belt where you have to pay for oxygen. Who knows why traffic control on this end even let them in the tunnel."

59

"Out of sight, out of mind," Ellen said philosophically. "Hey, this lasagna is really pretty good, but what does it have to do with the Ark?"

"So that's the one thing they did right. The cultists had brought three months of freeze-dried rations up on the space elevator, though they barely had enough water to last a week, and the Horten recycling system was meant for a crew of at most a dozen. Bad show all the way around, but a few of us who were in the area got the people off before they ran out of air. I happened to be almost two-thirds empty at the time so I managed to cram forty-six people into the cargo hold. Even though it was only a six-hour trip to the elevator hub on Four Sisters Prime, it took a month to get the smell out."

"That's awful. What happened to them?"

"The Drazens brought them down to the surface and put them to work so they could earn passage back to Earth. Those of us who were in on the rescue were awarded the Ark as salvage, so we split up all the freeze-dried food, and then somebody, I think it was Gary, towed the hulk into the tunnel and all the way to a Sharf recycling orbital. I found out later that he got a bonus from the Stryx for clearing a navigation hazard from a high-traffic area."

"Mountain Man Gary? The guy with the mouse living in his beard who runs the Tall Tales competition?"

"He only does the mouse thing at Rendezvous. Try the green beans."

"Thanks." Ellen moved some green beans to her plate and then took a second helping of lasagna. "You know what? I think that the Ark might have put the whole Colony One thing on the map. It got a lot of play in the Galactic Free Press. Even though the cult was a joke, the idea of humans wanting to start a new colony somewhere

60

rather than moving to established worlds with alien governments really resonated with some people. It's been almost a century since the Stryx opened Earth and we haven't done it yet."

"That's because we haven't developed our own interstellar drive and the Stryx don't connect tunnels to new systems until they're economically viable. Hey, did you hear that?"

"Was it barking? Do you think there are wild dogs around here?"

"If there are, I don't want to meet them, but it could be coyotes. My father said they were already a problem when he was still here."

"I'm going to get my stunner," Ellen said, rising from her place. "Back in a second."

"Me too."

The two returned to the table a few minutes later, each armed with a commercial-grade Dollnick stunner of the type favored by traders, and resumed their meal.

"So why don't the Stryx connect tunnels to promising systems as they're discovered?" Ellen asked. "I have to believe they would make their investment back in no time."

"You really don't know?" John paused with a forkful of green beans halfway to his mouth.

"Would I be asking if I did?"

"The only cost to the Stryx for opening new tunnels is the energy, and they seem to have infinite amounts of that. They wait until worlds are already terraformed and settled so they don't put the colony ship industry out of business. Even the Stryx-subsidized teacher bots we grew up with are programmed so they only share the knowledge that humanity has already discovered for itself. The Stryx

61

started the tunnel network to bring together the species that are willing to trade rather than fight, but they don't want to destroy any existing industries. The one thing that all the biological species have in common is that without work, we tend to make problems."

"My only problem is that you've been avoiding me the last few years."

"You know why that is, Ellen. I can't be around your drinking."

"I've cut back on the hard stuff—I don't even keep any on the ship anymore, except as trade stock."

John looked at the half-empty bottle of wine sadly. "Let's just say it didn't work out between us and leave it at that."

"I thought it was working out just fine."

Six

"Lorper Orbital administration requesting navigation handover," the ship's controller announced.

"Close the hatch to the cargo deck and proceed," Larry ordered the controller and looked over to see if the alarm buzzer would wake Georgia. "Are you still sleeping off that squeeze tube of baked scrod casserole?"

"I'm up, I'm up," the reporter said, opening her eyes and staring in horror at a long thread of spittle that was floating just inches in front of her face. "Is that mine?"

"I wanted you to see what happens if you sleep with your mouth open in Zero-G," Larry told her matter-of-factly. "Some traders who can't break the habit wear a cloth surgical mask while they sleep just to save having to clean it up."

"What if my drool had gotten into the electronics and shorted something out?"

"Humans couldn't live in space if the equipment was that fragile. Everything on the bridge is rated for tempo-rary submersion, but that doesn't mean saliva won't leave a sticky residue on the view screen. There's a story about a rookie trader who burned through an entire fuel pack making course changes to avoid a navigation hazard that stayed right in front of his ship throughout evasive action."

"You mean it was just gunk on the view screen? Did that really happen?"

"I doubt it. Traders tell lots of rookie stories like that, and the ship controller would have known better."

"Are there paper towels somewhere, or do you have a vacuum cleaner?"

"It's all vacuum outside. If you have a squeeze-tube disaster, we'll go into the hold and seal the hatch, and then the controller can vent the bridge atmosphere through a filter. Nobody complains about dumping gases in space." Larry corralled the long strand of free-floating spittle with a tissue, but instead of taking it to the garbage, he shoved it in a pocket and pulled himself back to his chair. "Buckle your safety harness for docking. It's a Drazen regulation."

"Got it. Hey, are we moving?"

"We've been moving for the last three days. You meant to ask if we're accelerating."

"My question stands."

"That's Lorper traffic control bringing us in with manipulator fields. None of the alien stations or orbitals allow ships to dock under the captain's control, there's just too much at stake. You slept through me giving up authority so the AI running Lorper could shut down all of our navigation controls and handle us directly."

"I didn't know the Drazens were big on AI."

"They're not, and some species actually handle traffic control with highly-trained technicians, but AI is a natural fit, and it's good-paying work for them when they need the money. I hear that gambling addictions are common with some types of artificial intelligence."

"Weird," Georgia commented. "Have you ever been here before?"

"I try to stop a few times a year. There's a large contingent of human contract workers, at least two million, and what with the families, they always need shoes."

"You deal in shoes? I thought you'd trade something high-tech, like, I don't know."

Larry gave her a minute to think before replying. "Earth's idea of high-tech would be obsolete in an alien museum exhibition of their pre-tunnel network days. We're really that far behind. And kids go through shoes pretty quick. I try to keep around a quarter of my capital invested in children's shoes and clothes because they're almost as good as cash. For the rest of my cargo, I play it by ear and try to increase value through bartering."

"Some of the restaurateurs I interviewed for articles on Union Station bought special ingredients from traders to supplement the staple crops grown on the ag decks."

"Food is risky for traders, especially if it doesn't keep. I'll carry seeds, or even root vegetables on occasion if I can get a good price. Anything edible is welcome at mining colonies, so canned food is always a good bet, but the truth is, I like dabbling in alien goods. My dad used to say I was just one notch above a treasure hunter."

"Treasure hunters are bad?"

"Well, they usually waste their lives searching for treasures without finding anything."

"Ooh, I think I need to use the bathroom."

"That's because traffic control is matching us up to the orbital's radial acceleration so it can set us down. As your weight returns, it feels like your bladder is getting squeezed, and—"

"I got it, I got it. How long will it be?"

"Just another minute or so, you can hold it. I bet we're already in the core."

"How come there's nothing on the view screen?"

"I left it off in case it makes you nauseous. Are you game?"

"Try me."

"Controller. Viewscreen on."

The large panel came to life with a view of parked spaceships and cargo handling equipment, all of it upside-down and slowly rotating away from them.

"Is this place constructed the same way as Union Station?" Georgia asked.

"All space habitats are, at least, they are if the inhabitants want to weigh something," Larry explained. "There's no technology for creating localized artificial gravity, so living in a giant centrifuge is the only option. A good-sized orbital like this one has an open core just like a Stryx station, though on a much smaller scale."

"I've never really understood the difference between an orbital and a space station."

"Different species use the terms any way they want, but the tunnel network standard is that space stations can be anywhere while orbitals have to orbit a planet or a star. You see how the deck isn't rotating past us anymore? That means traffic control has matched our velocity and will be setting us down any—" there was a gentle thud as the ship's landing gear made contact with the deck, "—second."

"That's it? I don't feel my normal weight. Can I go to the bathroom now?"

"Yes, but don't use the vacuum attachments. Just do your normal thing and it will flush automatically when you get up."

Georgia ripped off her safety harness and disappeared into the small bathroom while Larry stood up and stretched.

"Welcome back to Lorper, Captain Larry," an odd-sounding voice came through the trade ship's console.

"Your navigation controls will remain locked until departure. Please drop your ramp and stand by for boarding and customs inspection."

"On my way," Larry replied. "Georgia, I'm heading down to the cargo deck to meet the customs inspector. Controller, open hatch."

The alarm buzzer sounded again, and after descending a few rungs of the ladder, the trader took the rest of the distance in a fireman's slide. Then he made his way to the main hatch, which doubled as a ramp, and pressed the actuator button. As usual, the customs inspector was waiting by the time the ramp hit the deck.

"Is that you, Janice?" Larry called to the woman, whose face was hidden by the long visor on her official cap.

"You're in luck again, smuggler," Janice said, looking up with a smile. "I don't know how you always manage to arrive during my shift."

"I bribed a Drazen supervisor to tip me off."

"Big spender. Any banned drugs, banned weapons, or banned books?"

"Banned books?" Larry asked in surprise as the customs inspector moved past him into the hold. "That's a new one. Is there a list?"

"Gotcha," Janice said. "I'm eleven for eleven with that line so far today. Traders are so gullible."

"Takes one to know one," Larry retorted, as she played a hand-scanner over his netted-in-place cargo. "Don't you miss it at all?"

"Days at a time in Zero-G doing monotonous exercises? Eating out of squeeze tubes. Pissing into a—hello. Who's this?"

"Georgia Hunt, Galactic Free Press," the reporter introduced herself as she stepped away from the ladder.

"Janice. Inspector Number Sixty-One," the uniformed woman replied. "Were you going to declare her, Larry?"

"Georgia? She's just hitching a ride."

"All working press must register with the orbital's administration. I assume from the introduction that you aren't here on vacation, Miss Hunt."

"No, I'm working. I didn't know about registering."

"I can handle it right here," Janice said, returning the scanner to her belt and pulling out a small tab. "There's a hundred cred fee."

"A hundred creds? I don't even know how long we're going to be here."

"How about twenty?"

"Play nice, Janice," Larry scolded the inspector. "What do I owe you for the cargo?"

"Just the standard bribe, and I still have to look at the bridge."

"Go on up. I trust you."

"And your controller will be recording my every move, no doubt," the customs inspector said. She holstered her tab and started up the ladder.

"What was that all about?" Georgia whispered. "Is she really corrupt?"

"Janice? No, she's a good one. Used to run a family trader with her husband, but when the kids were both old enough for school, they decided to take ten years somewhere with a decent human population."

"So she was joking about the bribes?"

"Not exactly. The way the Drazens work customs here, they figure that the inspectors are all going to take bribes, so they pay them a low base rate, like waitstaff. This way they get the inspections done for cheap."

"But doesn't the government want to collect fees?"

"The orbital doesn't have a government, it's run by the Blue Star consortium. Some of the older tunnel network species, like the Dollnicks, build colony ships that can double as terraforming platforms, but the Drazens keep a couple of these terraforming orbitals that they tow into place as needed. Lorper has been on the job here for a few hundred years, though they only started hiring workers from Earth a couple decades ago."

"But what if you were actually bringing in something illegal?"

"Like banned books?" Larry asked. "That scanner hanging from her belt would catch most of what they really care about, and if you're worried about doomsday weapons, checking for them after we're parked in the core would be too late. That inspection would have been done remotely as soon as I turned the ship over to the local traffic control."

"All set," Janice announced, returning after just a few seconds on the bridge. She accepted a five-cred coin from Larry and slipped it in her belt pouch. "Why don't you stop by the café for a drink and say 'Hi' to Danny? I know he misses being up on all the latest trade rumors."

"I'll do that," Larry said. "Thanks for the clean bill of health."

"Is that it?" Georgia asked, after the customs inspector headed down the ramp. "I don't really have to register or go through immigration or anything?"

"The Drazens could care less if you decided to stay here for the rest of your life as long as you didn't cause problems. If you hung around bothering people and refused to work, one day you'd wake up and find yourself on a ship to somewhere else." He looked over to the Sharf bot. "Genie, let's get the net down from Section Three."

"I can help you," the reporter offered.

"You're here to do a job, so take care of that first, and if you have time afterward, I'll welcome any help you can give me."

"That's right. The seminar here is starting soon so I better find the exhibition hall. I'll fill you in when I get back."

Georgia looked out through the shimmering atmosphere retention field, the only thing separating the open landing deck of the cylindrical orbital's core from the vacuum of space, and shuddered. On Union Station, the landing bays on the core also featured atmosphere retention fields, but they were backed by giant bay doors that were closed when not in use. The curvature of the deck was much more pronounced than on a Stryx station, where the cylindrical structure's diameter was so large that you barely noticed it most of the time. She headed for a nearby spoke, which was the most logical place for a lift tube, and was rewarded with the sight of somebody just emerging through the sliding doors.

Georgia entered the newly arrived capsule and instructed the lift tube, "Exhibition Hall."

"Please provide your payment method," an artificial voice announced.

"What? You charge for the lift tubes on this orbital?"

"You could take the stairs if there were any. Residents use the infrastructure for free, guests are charged on a sliding scale. I don't detect a resident transponder on your person."

"I've got a programmable cred but I'm not slotting it without knowing how much this is going to cost."

"Please state your profession and average income per cycle."

"I'm an investigative journalist with the Galactic Free Press," Georgia said, brandishing her ID at the ceiling. "I'm here on a freelance assignment."

"Freelance? Never mind."

The lift tube capsule set off, and for a few seconds, the reporter felt her weight decrease, before it started going up again as they moved farther away from the core.

"What did you mean by that?" she demanded when her brain caught up with the last comment. "I'm not a charity case."

"No, you're freelance," the AI running the lift tube said agreeably. "Been there, done that. Now I stick with paying gigs."

"Like running lift tubes?"

"I got this job as an add-on when I negotiated the contract for traffic control. I could run this whole orbital on my spare capacity, and since I've got to be here to dock the ships anyway, it makes sense to bid on the smaller jobs as they come open."

"Could I ask who your creators are?"

"I'm a twentieth generation mutt and I've got better uses for my memory," the AI replied as the capsule halted and the doors slid open. "Exhibition hall is down the corridor on your left."

Georgia followed the AI's instructions and quickly located the hall. Large display panels to either side of the main doors announced, "Colony One Seminar. All are welcome." She frowned at the closed doors and checked the time on her heads-up display. Then one of the doors slid open and a couple of middle-aged women pushing a catering floater emerged.

"Excuse me," Georgia addressed them. "Are you here setting up for the Colony One seminar?"

"Breaking down, honey," the older woman replied. "Show was over almost an hour ago."

"But it's early, and I know I got the date right," the reporter protested, pointing at the information on the bottom of the display panel.

"It's past ten in the evening and we have to be going," the caterer said. "Whose clock are you on?"

"UHT – Universal Human Time."

"This is a Drazen orbital," the younger woman told her. "Better luck next time."

Georgia remained staring at the display panel for a full minute, but then the training she had put herself through by reading autobiographies of famous investigative journalists kicked in, and she circled back to the strip of pubs she had passed on the way to the exhibition hall. She picked one that wasn't blasting loud music and was rewarded immediately. More than half of the people sitting at the tables sported name tags and were perusing glossy pamphlets that were being shared around from swag bags with the distinctive Colony One logo. The reporter ordered a pitcher of beer at the bar and then carried it over to a table where there were two open chairs.

"Is this seat taken?" Georgia asked nobody in particular after failing to draw the attention of any of the seminar goers.

"Were you planning to drink all of that yourself?" a man across the table with an empty glass inquired.

"I'm a sucker for quantity discounts," she said, taking the seat since nobody objected. After pouring herself a short beer, she pushed the pitcher into the middle of the table where it didn't remain for more than a second. "I take it you guys all went to the seminar?"

"I'd reserve a place on the Colony One ship right now if I could, but they aren't selling," the woman seated directly to her right said. She appeared to be flushed, but Georgia couldn't tell whether it was from alcohol or the excitement of the presentation. "That doesn't look like a seminar nametag," the woman added, pointing to the reporter's ID, and then to her own, which identified her as Deborah.

"No, these are my press credentials. I'm with the Galactic Free Press," Georgia told them. "I came all the way here from Union Station to catch the seminar but I arrived too late."

"Tough break," said the first man who had helped himself to her beer and whose nametag identified him as Tom. "I can tell you that they sold me."

"Sold you what, Tom?" Georgia asked eagerly.

"On the importance of humanity acquiring a colony ship and finding our own world somewhere. I'd heard rumors that EarthCent is working with the Drazens on some project to help us develop an interstellar drive, but even if we had one tomorrow, building a colony ship would take generations."

"And don't forget about all of the terraforming equipment, the gravity-drive shuttles, and all of the other scientific breakthroughs we haven't made yet," Deborah said. "I like the Dollnick colony ships," she added, speaking directly to Georgia. "There's already one hiring itself out to EarthCent, you know, but it's some kind of special circumstance that doesn't involve colonization. This booklet has pictures of all the colony ship types built by tunnel network members. You can keep it, I have two."

"Thank you," Georgia said. "It looks like an expensive printing job. How much did they charge?"

"These are all giveaways. There was a bag full of litera-ture on every seat when we went in, but the kid next to me said that he only reads on tabs. Here, you can have the whole bag. I just didn't want to see it go to waste."

"That's very generous of you. Everything was included with the entry fee then?"

"I only paid six creds to get in, and that included the meal at the end," Tom said.

"Yeah, the food itself had to cost that much. They must have gotten the hall for free or something," another man joined in.

"I waited in the corridor to talk with the last speaker," said a slender woman whose nametag identified her as Isabel. "I wanted to make a contribution, but Farsight said they weren't set up to accept cash."

"Farsight?" Georgia asked.

"That's his nom de guerre," Isabell explained. "He wanted to take a name that meant something."

"I don't really know much about them because they haven't visited Union Station," the reporter said. "I'm working on a story—"

"That's great," Tom interrupted. "They need all the pub-licity they can get if we're going to make this work. Colony One hasn't even started fundraising yet, but when they do, it's going to take trillions of creds. When you think about it, if every human worker in the galaxy just pledged a month or two of their earnings, we'd get there in no time."

"And you're ready to do that?" Georgia asked, belatedly pulling out her tab and opening the story-builder screen.

"You can quote me on it."

Seven

The sprawling commercial center at the base of the North American continent's space elevator was occupied primarily by wholesalers, exporters, and outfitters. A young boy showed Ellen how she could bring up an interactive map on the screen of the communications device she had purchased to contact journalists whose stories had been previously syndicated in the Galactic Free Press. She guessed that whoever was in charge of keeping the map up to date must have been on vacation because it still took her an hour to locate the fairgrounds set aside for small traders.

"Now I know why they call you a sell phone," she barked at the device, which for some reason showed her current location as a parking garage for floaters. "I'll sell you the first chance I get."

"That's cell phone, with a C," a man sitting cross-legged on a blanket a few steps away informed her. "Are you lost?"

"I was looking for a place to spread my blanket and do a little trading, but this map function decided to give me a grand tour of the area instead," Ellen replied. "So why do they call this thing a cell-phone-with-a-C?"

"It's short for cellular telephone, and the connectivity is supplied by antennas on cellular towers. The problem is that the space elevator interferes with the location signal for miles around. Your first time here?"

"My first time on Earth. I'm meeting some people here today and I hope it's not as hard for them to find the fairgrounds as it was for me."

"As long as they've been here before they'll know about the map thing, and who hasn't visited the space elevator? It's also the main transportation hub on the East Coast."

"That's why I picked it," Ellen said. "I was told that all roads, rails, and sub-orbital flights lead to the space elevator. Is that spot next to you open?" she added, pointing at a patch of artificial grass. "I only brought what's in my pack."

"Make yourself at home," the trader said. "I'm Marshall, and the fairground charges six creds a day for a blanket rental."

"I have a blanket," Ellen said, shrugging her way out of the bulky pack and then kneeling to undo the main flap. "Right on top here. See?"

"I meant they charge six creds a day to spread your blanket. That's why I called it a rental."

"What do we get for the six creds?"

"Left alone. The collector bot wanders through every half-hour or so, and if you refuse to pay, it sprays you and your goods with water-based paint. Nobody messes with it."

"Are you sure the bot works for the elevator authority and not some bright kid who put it together to extort rent from traders?"

"What difference does it make? Everybody has to pay somebody, and six creds a day is reasonable enough. Are you here with your ship?"

"It's in Lot K," Ellen told him.

"The ETA didn't tell you about the long-term lot for traders?"

"The who?"

"Elevator Transit Authority. They handle all of the incoming traffic for the elevator."

"I spent a few days at some little town upstate and then flew here without returning to orbit."

"The long-term lot is sponsored by EarthCent, and in addition to being half the price, you get all of the hookups, like a campground. It's a little farther out, but there's a monorail."

"Thanks. I'll move my ship there this evening."

Ellen spread her blanket and began setting out the goods from her pack. For the sake of maximizing value at a manageable weight, she had brought ten disposable Dollnick stunners in retail packaging, plus a half-dozen large tablecloths woven with a proprietary Frunge semi-metallic process.

Marshall let out a long whistle and commented, "Pricey. The stunners might sell for twenty creds, but you won't see many shoppers who can afford those tablecloths. That's boutique stuff on Earth."

"I paid thirty creds cash for these stunners on Union Station, and that was direct from a wholesaler."

"They used to go for fifty around here, easy, but lots of traders started showing up with them a month or two back and the price collapsed. I stick with the basics when I come to Earth."

Ellen took a minute to go over and study her helpful neighbor's offerings. She saw that he was selling alien drama series in a variety of storage formats, a selection of blank Horten holocubes which she suspected were factory seconds, and hundreds of bubble packs of pills labeled in Farling.

"The local authorities don't give you grief about selling meds?" she asked.

"Nobody comes around to check, and besides, everybody knows the Farling stuff works as advertised. Anti-hangover pills are my biggest seller, and I traded for those green ones just before coming to Earth. They're supposed to cure the common cold."

"How about anti-intoxication pills?"

"You want to drink alcohol and not get drunk? Are you a card sharp?"

"I just have a little trouble stopping once I get started," Ellen admitted.

"I've heard that the Gem sell nanobots that could do the job, but they probably cost a fortune and they can't last that long in the body. A Farling doctor could probably fix you up, they're supposedly the best in the galaxy, but I don't know where you'd find one. In the meantime, take a pack of these anti-hangover pills, on the house."

"And they're your biggest seller?"

"Paid my blanket rental ten minutes after I got here," Marshall asserted, tossing her a bubble pack. "Maybe I was wrong about those tablecloths, it looks like you have a prospect."

Ellen turned back to her own blanket and saw a couple of well-dressed women crouching on their heels to examine one of the tablecloths.

"What lovely fabric," the older woman remarked. "How much is it?"

"Those are genuine Frunge-weave, from the colony on Tzeba Four," Ellen launched into her pitch. "You can see that it's woven from individually dyed threads, not a print, and the—"

"Price?" the younger woman interrupted.

"In a boutique on Union Station, these tablecloths sell for over a hundred creds."

"We aren't on Union Station and there's a trader with a whole load of them at the other end of the fairgrounds selling for forty-five creds."

"Forty-five? That doesn't make any sense. Wholesale on these is forty-eight to fifty, depending on the pattern, and there's only one source."

"So your usual mark-up is a hundred percent?"

"I was going to offer one to you for eighty creds," Ellen said. "Do you have any idea how much it costs to operate as a solo trader? My mortgage—"

"Isn't our problem," the older woman cut her off. "Good luck finding some shoppers with more money than sense. Are those the new cold pills?" she continued, turning to Ellen's neighbor.

"Straight from Farling Pharmaceuticals," Marshall confirmed. "Six creds per pack."

"That's so reasonable," the younger woman enthused. "I'll take two."

"And I'll take three," her companion said.

Ellen watched as the other trader handed over five bubble packs and collected thirty creds. He gave her a wink, and then she jumped like a startled rabbit when something began vibrating her right butt cheek.

"Stupid cell phone," she growled when she realized what it was, and then almost fumbled it to the ground. "Why can't Earthers get implants like everybody else?"

"There's no infrastructure to support implant communication functions here," Marshall answered, even though she had intended the question as rhetorical. The phone vibrated again as Ellen was trying to unlock the screen, and this time she did drop it. "You can change it to an audible ringtone, you know."

"Right after I take this," she said, bending over and successfully tracing out her lock-code on the screen with the device still resting on the blanket. "Hello?"

"This is Bryan Livingston. I'm at the fairgrounds. Can you push me your location?"

"Do what?"

"Here," Marshall offered, stepping into the narrow green margin between their blankets. "I'll enable it for you."

"Just a sec," she told Bryan and handed over the phone. "I thought you said the elevator messed up the location signal."

"It's the timing of the satellite signals that the elevator stalk alters," the trader said, swiping and tapping at the screen. "Location push is a direct function, phone-to-phone. It will run your battery down in just a couple hours if you leave it on continuously, but it works anywhere because it's based on signal strength. See the blinking blue dot on the screen?"

"Is that him?"

"Yup. You're in the bottom right corner by default, don't ask me why. You can monitor his progress if you want."

"He'll get here when he gets here. Do I need to leave the call open?"

"No, you can hang-up. It's a completely different function."

Ellen watched enviously as Marshall sold a hundred seasons of an old Vergallian drama to another customer for five times what it would have cost her to buy a legitimate copy on any Stryx station. The same guy turned his nose up at her disposable stunners when she offered one at break even.

"No thanks," the drama addict rejected her offer. "There's a woman selling them for twenty-five over by the exotic pets section and she's throwing in free holsters."

"I don't understand," Ellen complained to Marshall. "How can the traders here be selling goods below cost?"

"Maybe they got them in some sweet barter deals and now they're just cashing out," the other trader said. "I'm the old-fashioned type, so when I'm looking to acquire stock, I always go for the best value rather than gambling on hot sellers. I've noticed lately that quite a few of the younger Guild members are crowding into the same trades."

"Are you going to Rendezvous this year?"

"Never missed one yet, and there's the election this time around to boot. It's about time we get representation with the Conference of Sovereign Human Communities. I'm always surprised when traders tell me they're going to vote for anti-CoSHC candidates, and the same people are pushing giving the vote to non-owner operators."

"That I don't get at all," she agreed. "It would turn the Traders Guild into an organization of delivery pilots."

"Ellen?" inquired a tall man who was holding a cell phone level in front of himself like a compass.

"Bryan? Pleased to meet you."

"Are you selling these?" Bryan asked, picking up one of the Dollnick retail packs. "I've been thinking about starting to carry a stunner on the job."

"I paid thirty creds wholesale, but there's someone here selling them for twenty-five," Ellen informed him reluctantly. "I can let you have one for that."

"How about two? My wife reports on local politics and things are getting a bit heated in our area."

"Two for fifty," she agreed. "How was your trip in?"

"It's just an hour and a half by floater on auto-pilot. I belong to AirShare so it's cheaper than renting. You said that you're scouting freelancers for the Galactic Free Press?"

"Yes, in part. I've been contacting all of your colleagues who used to work for the news syndicates and had articles picked up by my paper. If you have anything you're working on right now, I can put you in touch with the head of the freelance department, but my real job here is to convince you to organize a new syndicate. My bosses would rather work with one group than manage hundreds of new freelancers."

"A number of us have been discussing setting up our own syndicate, but we're still trying to work out how to finance the office and support staff with enough left over to make a living," Bryan told her. "Most of us do some work for the local rags, primarily sports reporting or politics, but aside from the main daily in a few of the big city-states, none of the papers have the readership to pay for investigative journalism."

"That's what my boss figured. I don't want you to think that I'm here handing out candy, but if you can put together a convincing business plan, the Galactic Free Press may be willing to help subsidize your launch," Ellen told him.

"Just like that?" the journalist replied skeptically. "If we set up as a new syndicate, that means we'll be selling the same stories to your potential competitors."

"I'm just a freelancer they tapped for this job, not management."

"You know, I wouldn't have agreed to see you if I hadn't read your story about the longevity scam. That was a fine piece of reporting."

"And I really appreciate that you're here," Ellen said. "I hate talking over that cell phone, and none of the other journalists from your old syndicate were willing to come, even though I'm pretty sure some of them lived closer than you."

"They delegated me," Bryan said. "Everybody is scrambling to make a living, and there was no point in all of us coming if you were really here to pitch us some scheme where we pay you to get our stories published."

"Is that even a thing?"

"It is on Earth. Some of the papers that used to buy our syndication feed replaced us with vanity news."

"People writing about themselves?"

"Pretty much. A chunk of what goes in the local papers was always press releases from businesses or stories rewritten from the student teacher-bot news. But lately there are more and more people who write articles about themselves or something they're involved in, and then pay to get the stories published. Vanity news."

"But who would want to read that?"

"The papers don't care because they make their money upfront."

"I guess the press on Earth must be pretty desperate," Ellen said. "I suppose the free version of the Galactic Free Press isn't helping."

"No, but people here who care about the news mainly watch the Children's News Network or read the student papers on teacher bots. It's hard to compete with a billion connected kids who are reporting on the spot. The truth is, most people on Earth choose to watch the Grenouthian news with all the immersive content of things blowing up around the galaxy."

"Well, at least that explains why you're the only person from the defunct North American news syndicate who agreed to my invitation. I've got meetings with three more journalists scheduled, but they're all coming in from different continents later on sub-orbital flights."

"Maybe I could get together with them after you make your pitch," Bryan said. "First I should find a little privacy somewhere and conference with my colleagues to see how they want me to respond to your offer. We pretty much assumed that you were just here looking for a cheap source of Earth content, but your proposition deserves serious discussion. How long will you be around?"

"I'm on the planet for another three weeks, and then I'm heading to Rendezvous. If there's a reason to come back after that, I will, as long as I can come to terms with my boss. I'm freelance too, you know."

Bryan paid for the two stunners, slipped them into his shoulder bag, and headed off to find a place to sit down and contact the other journalists he was representing. Ellen settled cross-legged on the blanket to hawk her wares and wait for her next meeting. A number of shoppers stopped by, and she sold two more stunners at a loss, but nobody was biting on an eighty-cred tablecloth, and she was unwilling to go any lower on what she still considered prime merchandise.

"If I wasn't getting paid by the Galactic Free Press to be here, I'd be in the red myself," she admitted to Marshall during a long lull. "I checked the Advantage platform before I left Union Station, and it said that those disposable stunners and tablecloths were a sure thing."

"I've never heard of Advantage, but maybe it's why there are so many traders here selling the same merchandise," her neighbor pointed out. "If you look now, it could be saying the opposite."

"Advantage is a trading conditions platform I joined, but I don't know how to access it without a Stryxnet connection," Ellen said. "I wish Earth had modern communications infrastructure."

"Give your phone here and I'll see if I can bring it up and set a ringtone for you at the same time," Marshall said. "Do you have a favorite song?"

"Anything is fine," she replied, unlocking the cell phone and handing it over. The older man confidently worked his way through the byzantine menus and eventually managed to bring up the Advantage portal.

"You have to enter your account information and password," he said, handing the phone back.

"It better still be my name and my ship registration number or I'm not going to know it," Ellen said, filling in the required fields. "Hey, it worked. Let me see if I can find—I can't believe it."

"What?"

"The screen came up on the Earth market right away, I guess since it's the last one I looked at. They're still showing disposable Dollnick stunners as the top recommendation for trade stock."

"Can't you post a correction?"

"It doesn't work that way. I can only edit the cargo in my own profile, and they have an algorithm that sorts everything and presents the most profitable cargo suggestions based on the wisdom of crowds."

"Maybe they're using the wisdom of clowns."

"Very funny. Look," she said, brandishing the phone in front of Marshall's nose. "They're still recommending Frunge tablecloths in the top-ten list as well."

"Are you sure they aren't making recommendations to you based on what you've reported in your inventory?"

"No, I bought the stunners and the tablecloths after seeing the recommendation. It's part of the research I'm doing for a story. Wait a second, I'm going to try something." Ellen input a search term and surveyed the result grimly. "Not recommended," she reported. "Apparently there's an oversupply of Farling medicine for sale on Earth."

"I wouldn't put much faith in their suggestions if I was you." Marshall cast a quick look around to see if anybody was nearby before continuing. "I don't normally go around spreading rumors, but it seems to me that I'm hearing about more young traders who have been running into financial problems lately. Maybe there's a relationship there."

The phone suddenly played the opening bars to the first movement of Beethoven's Fifth symphony. She closed the portal and accepted the call. "Ellen here."

"Maria Cortez. I'm at the fairgrounds. Could you push me your location?"

"Just a sec," she responded, and passed the phone back to Marshall. This time he made sure she was watching as he invoked the homing signal. "She's practically on top of us," Ellen said, lifting her head and scanning the area. "That must be her looking down at the phone."

A minute later, a woman with a travel bag slung over one shoulder approached and asked, "Are you Ellen?"

"And you're Maria. Pleased to meet you," Ellen said, and the two women exchanged a polite handshake.

"Do I have permission to step on your blanket?"

"Please. I'm not one of those old-fashioned traders who takes it so seriously."

"I've come a long way so I hope this isn't some trick to sell me expensive tablecloths," the journalist said. "A bunch of us who are in the same shoes pooled the money for my ticket."

"Funny, the reporter I just met was also representing a group. Saves work for me, I guess."

"So, the Galactic Free Press is taking an interest in our little revolution in the Southern Hemisphere?"

"I didn't know you were having one, but if it's not a weekly occurrence, I'm sure you can sell the story to the freelance desk. Do you really have so many people left down there that they're still fighting over natural resources?"

"Do you count greed as a natural resource?"

"Point taken."

Eight

"Is it me, or is it warmer in here than it was during our last trip?"

"I visit Verlock open worlds whenever I get the chance so I guess I'm pretty insensitive to temperature," Larry said. "Controller, run the environmental diagnostic check."

"Test failed," the artificial voice came back almost immediately. "Problem detected in the secondary cooling system."

"Is that bad?" Georgia asked.

"It's not good," Larry replied, and began unbuckling the complicated harness that made working out on the rock climbing machine feel somewhat realistic.

"Your controller did say that it was the secondary system so we still have the primary. Right?"

"The primary system cools the thrusters and the equipment. The secondary system cools us."

"I would have thought that heat would be more important. Isn't it absolute zero in space?"

"We're not in space, we're in my ship," Larry said, and launched himself towards the hatch that led to the cargo deck. "Coming?"

"I don't get it," she said, pushing off gently to follow. "I just assumed all this time that we weren't freezing because the ship was keeping us warm."

"Do you know the three ways that heat is transferred?"

"When something hot touches something cold, the heat flows to the cold until they're the same temperature."

"That's conduction, and the controlling factor is mass. The reason the hull of the ship isn't at absolute zero is because space is a vacuum. Other than a few gas atoms, there's no mass to conduct the heat away. The second type of heat transfer is convection, which means an actual flow and mixing of material, like cold air blown into a room filled with warm air."

"I guess we wouldn't want to open a window."

"You guessed right. The final type of heat transfer is radiation, like sunshine. If we turned off all of the equipment on board, including ourselves, the heat left in the ship would eventually radiate away, but it takes a long time. Since we can't turn ourselves off without dying in the process, fixing the secondary cooling system is now my top priority." He shuffled from the ladder to a large grey locker and removed a belt with a number of tools attached to small spring-loaded reels. "This is the tool locker, by the way."

"Can I do anything to help?" she asked.

"The technical deck on these Sharf traders is below the cargo hold, and it's pretty cramped because it's not intended for in-flight service. I'm going to have to wedge myself in there so I'd appreciate if you could be my outside hands. Got your magnetic cleats on?"

"Yeah, I learned my lesson there." Georgia clicked her heels to activate the cleats and then shuffled after her captain

"The best access to the technical deck is right by the main hatch since that's the last place anybody would store cargo. Some traders go nuts carrying bulk commodities and they have to climb over their own load just to get to the bridge, but I like to keep the area clear for emergencies."

Larry bent over and turned a small handle recessed into the deck. Then he shuffled a few paces further and bent again to release another manual lockout. Finally, he moved to the midpoint of the access panel and felt around the edge for a small depression. When he pulled up, a steel sheet almost as large as the main display screen came free, and he carefully maneuvered it into position against the inside of the hatch.

"Aren't you worried that will fall on you?" Georgia asked, after Larry turned his back on the removed access panel and reached for the edge of the opening.

"No gravity," he reminded her. "It's not going anywhere." He pulled a flashlight from his belt and shined the beam in the narrow space under the decking. "I don't smell anything. Do you?"

"Just us," Georgia said. "Do they add something stinky to make it easy to locate leaks?"

"Yes, but it's only stinky to the Sharf, though those dogs Joe has back on Union Station can sniff out a leak from across the hold. That's what I don't get about this. It was fine last week."

"Wasn't the hold more crowded when we started?"

"You finally noticed," Larry said, letting go of the flashlight, which was pulled back to his belt by the reel. "While you were drinking in bars or whatever it is investigative journalists do, I got rid of all of those salad containers I've been trying to unload."

"What did you trade them for?" Georgia asked, having caught on from his conversation that the captain was a fan of barter.

"Cash, but I needed it to cover the mortgage anyway. Controller, turn on the technical deck emergency lights." A blue glow came from the opening, and he grabbed the edges and began to pull himself under the decking.

"Why blue?"

"Original Sharf lights. It takes getting used to but the color actually makes it easier to—what the?!"

"What?"

"Somebody sabotaged me," Larry said angrily, and although his upper body was now hidden from her, Georgia could just imagine the look on his face. "A chewer has been at the hoses in here."

"You mean like a rat?"

"A mechanical chewer, basically a small bot. It wouldn't be able to get through any of the alloys the Sharf use for the critical systems, but the secondary cooling unit uses flexible hoses, and something has been at them."

"Can you fix it?"

"Sure, but the damn chewer will just be at it again as soon as I replace the access panel, and I only carry enough refrigerant for one full recharge." Larry squirmed back into open space and sat up. "Did anybody give you a package to deliver to a friend or anything like that?"

"What? No. And even if somebody had smuggled a thing like that on board, how would it get down there?"

"A chewer is small enough to fit through the vents. Maybe it got mixed in with the cargo somehow," he added. "I do trade for household goods, and it's not like I have enemies lined up around the galaxy waiting for a chance to do me in."

"Somebody could be trying to stop me from writing about Colony One."

"Have you been going around announcing that you think it's a scam?"

"I'm not that stupid. So what are we going to do?"

"Genie," Larry called for the cargo handling bot.

Georgia turned to watch as the Sharf bot emerged from its charging bay and floated over to where Larry was still sitting in the opening to the technical deck.

"You're going to set a bot to catch a bot?"

"First we've got to find it," Larry said. "Genie, there's an invasive bot onboard that's already damaged the secondary cooling system. Can you detect any motion?"

The boxy alien bot turned slowly through three hundred and sixty degrees. "There is an unidentified power source moving beneath the deck plating behind the primary thruster. Correction. The device is identified as a maintenance chewer for residential drain cleaning. Corrective action should be taken immediately."

"I want you to continually track the chewer's location starting now, so if it shuts down to hide, we'll know it's still at the last location you detected," Larry instructed. He turned to his passenger. "Were you serious about not being claustrophobic?"

"Yes. I was always hiding in small spaces and reading books my parents didn't approve of when I was a child."

"I can't work my way under the deck to where the chewer is without disassembling half of the ductwork. If need be, we can shift the cargo and start removing more access panels, but if the chewer keeps moving, I'll end up having to take half of the hold apart."

"So you're asking me if I can go under there and catch it?"

"Only if you're completely comfortable," Larry said. "If there's any chance you're going to freak out and get stuck, it's better not to try."

"No, I'll do it, but what about the chewer? Is it dangerous?"

"Chewers are pretty common on worlds where aggressive roots grow out of the sewer system and work their way into household drains. They're small enough that you can put them down the sink, and they'll chew their way until the drain is clear, or they start running out of juice and have to return. I suppose it makes sense that it went after the hoses."

"So it's, like, smaller than my fist?"

"Much smaller, and it doesn't have a mouth, just a rotating bit like you'd see on a rig for drilling wells, only miniature. Picture a metal cockroach with three tiny rotating spiky balls for a head."

"That doesn't sound so bad," Georgia said. "Can I have your flashlight?"

"Sure." Larry detached the reel from his belt and passed the whole unit to her, then moved to one end of the opening. "I'll stay down here so I can watch you, and if there's any problem at all, you—"

"Don't worry, I'm not the heroic type," she told him, clipping the reel to her sleeve and pulling herself into the opening. "Which way?"

"Do you see that little funnel cloud of black dust?"

"What is it?"

"Ground up hose that hasn't dispersed because there's limited air movement down here."

"Why is it shaped that way?"

"Probably has to do with the way the refrigerant gas leaked out. Anyway, you want to go around the other side of the coils, not through the dust, and then it's a straight shot to the main thrusters. I'll give you an update when you get there."

"Got it," the reporter said, and began to work her way through the cramped space by gently pulling her way forward on whatever she could reach. "I'd hate to have to do this if I weighed something."

"You've taken to Zero-G like a duck to water," Larry encouraged her. "Genie, any update on the chewer location?"

"The maintenance chewer is still moving behind the primary thruster, heading towards the primary cooling exchanger."

"You're going to cut it off at the pass," Larry called to the girl. "You know, I don't think it could be an accident after all. The chewer couldn't be moving around in Zero-G unless somebody intentionally magnetized the legs. I'll bet it's programmed to move really slowly to avoid losing contact with whatever surface it's sticking to."

"So you're saying if I pick it up like a lobster, it will be helpless."

"If it's anything like the size of a lobster, I want you to get out of there." He changed his position in an attempt to be able to follow Georgia's progress. "Looks like you're almost there."

"I think I see the inside of the hull right in front of me. I'm checking both directions and—gross!"

"What's wrong?"

"Nothing. It's just that it really does look like a cockroach. We always got them in the commune kitchen because everybody wanted to cook and not clean."

"It's just a little dumb bot."

"I know." There was a moment of silence, and then a distinctive crunching sound was heard.

"Are you all right?"

"I think I killed it," the reporter called back. "I meant to just pick it up, but it felt so gross that I kind of squeezed too hard."

"That's even better," Larry said. "Do you have room to turn around?"

"No problem. I'll be out in a few minutes."

"Okay. I'm going to start gathering the parts I need to make the repairs. I'll bet it was able to hold onto the hose because of the curvature, but it got blown off when the leak started."

By the time Georgia pulled herself out of the technical deck crawl-space, Larry had gathered everything he hoped he would need to do the repair in a work bag to keep it all from floating off.

"Good job," he praised the reporter when she showed him the remains of the chewer. "Genie, is the power source dead?"

"The maintenance chewer's fuel cell is in open circuit mode."

"What does that mean?" Georgia asked.

"You crunched it good so that there's no longer a complete circuit," Larry said. "Maybe you should keep it to show your friends when you tell the story of how you saved a spaceship. I've got some Dollnick crystal glue somewhere so you could seal it into a clear pendant for a necklace."

Georgia surprised both of them by blushing. "Thanks. I'm a regular big game hunter. I'll hang around out here to fetch and carry for you while you're fixing the cooler."

"Dinner's on me next time we're somewhere with a restaurant," Larry said, pulling himself back under the cargo deck and setting to work replacing the damaged hoses.

"Those people I was talking to in the bar might have guessed that I'm investigating Colony One from the questions I was asking," Georgia mused out loud. "One of them may have slipped the chewer into my purse or even the bag of promotional brochures. It's so small I might have missed it."

"I don't know," Larry replied after a minute. "Why would any of them have been carrying a chewer with magnetized legs? They could hardly have been expecting you."

"Well, you said you don't have any enemies."

"I said I don't have enemies lined up around the galaxy, but that's not the same thing as none. There's a Traders Guild election coming up, and I'm standing for the council this year as a candidate for the CoSHC faction in place of my father, who's the outgoing council head. Some traders are getting pretty worked up about the election, which sort of took us all by surprise."

"You're joining the Conference of Sovereign Human Communities? I've been to one of their conventions on Union Station and it's all representatives from human communities on alien open worlds and orbitals. What does it have to do with the Traders Guild?"

"They invited us to join," Larry explained, and then paused to examine his work. "If you add up all of the independent traders, there are more of us than the population of most CoSHC members, and it's about time we had some representation. Hang on a sec while I refill this thing, I need to pay attention."

Georgia waited patiently for a minute, and then she heard a hissing sound that started fairly loud, but quickly ran down until it was inaudible.

"What was that? Did it leak?"

"No, that was just the system refilling. It should be all set now. I'm coming out."

"But what if it did leak? You said you only had enough for one recharge. Will we cook before we get out of the tunnel?"

"We might have had to back off exercise and sit around naked, but it wouldn't have gotten that bad in just two days," Larry told her. "There's also an emergency tap on the primary cooling system I could have temporarily hooked up to, but that's a lot of work."

"Do all traders know as much about their ships as you do?"

Larry pulled himself out of the crawl space, gave his work bag a gentle push in the direction of the tool locker, and reached for the access panel. "Half and half, maybe? The majority of our traders fly second-hand Sharf ships, primarily the two-man version, because there happened to be hundreds of thousands of them available cheap when the Stryx opened Earth. Believe it or not, the Guild got its start when a bunch of first-generation traders got together to publish a sort of repair and maintenance manual for the systems that humans are capable of fixing. But not everybody is a mechanic."

"Why didn't the ship controller warn us when the leak started?"

"It's not considered a critical system and I turned off the secondary alarms years ago," Larry admitted as he locked down the access panel. "I got tired of the controller waking me up to tell me that the toilet receptacle was ready to be emptied or that it was time to lubricate the main hatch hinge. Now I just review the alert queue once a day on my tab."

Georgia watched as Larry put away the tools. "So when is the Traders Guild election?"

"A little over three more weeks, at the end of Rendezvous. If you haven't wrapped up your Colony One investigation before then, you'll have to take a break or go it alone for a couple weeks."

"Where is Rendezvous this year?" she asked, following him onto the ladder.

"At a Vergallian Fleet open world on a brand new tunnel exit the Stryx recently opened. There was a lot of arguing about that too."

"What do traders have against it?"

"The gravity and the atmosphere. Some traders fly ships that are patched together junk with just enough thrust to travel the tunnel network between space stations and elevator hubs. They hate it when Rendezvous is on a planet. Do you want to try the rock climber?"

"I'll stick with the bike," Georgia said, launching herself towards the now-familiar exercise equipment. "So who chose the location?"

"The human community there made a deal with the Vergallians to offer free space elevator transportation for attendees. The Guild council thought it would be too rude to refuse."

"Maybe I can get a story out of Rendezvous, though I'll bet the Galactic Free Press is already sending somebody. Hey, I should contact them from our next stop and tell them I'm going. Maybe they'll give me the assignment."

"Did you have any luck with the squeeze tube cuisine story you submitted from Lorper?"

"I didn't tell you? They bought it, and the message from my old editor was that she'd take all the Zero-G dining stories I can write, at least until I start repeating myself. But after we ate in your friend's café on Lorper, I had an idea for a more cerebral series of articles about why people eat the way they do in different places. I'm going to title it 'Food for Thought.'"

"I think the freelance life is starting to agree with you."

"Me too. I can't believe how fast I'm getting used to everything. This is only my third time on the exercise bike and it's already gotten much easier."

"Lesson two," Larry said. "The dial with the numbers sets the resistance. It's considered polite to leave equipment on the easiest setting when you're sharing, so I turned it down after I used it."

"Oops."

"You didn't know because I didn't tell you. Later I'll show you how to empty the toilet receptacle."

"I'm fine with you doing it. I don't want you to think I'm trying to take over your ship."

Nine

"Myort, you old lizard. I've been looking all over the station for you."

"John," the Huktra acknowledged. He set his mug full of some tarry black beverage on the bar and politely offered the trader a clawed hand. The human grasped the smallest of the three fingers, which was as thick as a child's wrist, and gave it a perfunctory shake. Formalities disposed of, he climbed up the rungs of the barstool next to the alien and perched himself on the broad seat.

"I just got back from Earth and I brought you a little gift," John said. He stuck his left hand into his jacket pocket, brought out a closed fist, and placed it on the bar. Then he opened his hand and let the acorn roll out. "Surprise!"

The Huktra slammed his own hand over the acorn so hard that his talons dug into the bar's heavily scarred surface. The bartender glanced over at the sound, shook his head in disgust, and went back to polishing glasses.

"Are you insane showing that thing in here?" Myort hissed. He bared two rows of pointy teeth and took advantage of his sinuous neck to check their surroundings in three hundred and sixty degrees. "No sniffers. We lucked out."

"I think my translation implant is glitching," John said. "What are you talking about?"

"You've traded in and around our space. Are you telling me you've never noticed that some of us have long snouts?"

"I've never seen a Huktra with a short snout."

Myort shook his head in disgust, and then, with a quick movement, palmed the crushed acorn and tossed it deep in his mouth to where the molars started. He chewed for a few seconds, then took a swig of his drink and swished it around. "Not terrible, not great. How many do you have?"

"How many do you want?" John countered.

"Oh, so it's going to be *that* sort of trade," the alien said. "Let me buy you a drink."

"Do they have anything in here that won't kill me?"

"We won't know unless we ask. Gator!"

The alien bartender, who John would have described as a skinnier version of Myort, hung the glass he had just finished polishing from an overhead rack and cast a disinterested look in their direction. "What?"

"Got anything that won't kill Humans?" Myort inquired.

"Water," the bartender grunted. "I could put a little umbrella in it."

"Never mind," John said. "Why don't you finish your drink, Myort, and we can go look at the merchandise."

"Are you in a big hurry to unload your cargo?" the alien asked craftily, but he threw back the rest of the sticky fluid and employed his long tongue to lick out the mug. "I'm a bit short on cash at the moment, but I'll look at what you have."

"Look at what I have? I was talking about us taking a stroll to wherever your ship is parked and me checking out if you have anything I want in barter."

"Barter is better," Myort responded automatically. "All right, we'll do it your way," he said, rising from the barstool and tossing a coin to the bartender. "See you later, Gator."

Gator barely nodded as the mismatched pair left the bar and made their way to the nearest lift tube. The corridor was lined with food booths, all of which seemed to specialize in selling grilled meat on sticks. There were also a few shops displaying woven egg carriers in the garish colors favored by young Huktra couples, who were much more likely to spend time on Stryx stations than their elders.

"Keever's," Myort instructed the lift tube, and looked down at John. "Got your nose plug filters?"

"They're already in. The trick is remembering to breathe through them. Why aren't you parked in the core bay for traders?"

"Getting a little work done on my ship. You'll see."

The capsule doors opened and the large alien led the way through a poorly lit corridor to a medium-sized docking bay. Even with nose plug filters, the air smelled of chemicals, and John could see flexible fume-hood tubing crisscrossing the space between the parked ships.

"What is this place?" he asked his companion.

"Keever's hull shop, they specialize in custom paint jobs," Myort explained. "Oh, now that's just—Wrude!"

"You don't have to shout. What's rude?"

"Wrude is the name of the Dollnick finish artist I hired. I can't believe what he did to her eyes," the Huktra complained.

"Whose eyes? What are you talking about?"

"Don't you recognize my ship? Look at the prow," the alien said, pointing with a claw.

John had to crane his neck to see the tip of the Huktra freighter, which was four times the size of the standard two-man Sharf trader most humans favored. "That's some beautiful artwork," he said. "Somebody you know?"

"My wife, if I can ever get her to engrave her signature in the tablet," Myort said. "Look what Wrude did to her baby reds."

"Are you talking about the eyes? They're green."

"Now you're catching on. Wrude!"

Nobody ignores the bellowing of a Huktra for long, and a Dollnick wearing a paint-splattered apron hurried over, looking annoyed.

"What is it now, Myort?" the four-armed alien demanded in an angry whistle that almost overloaded John's translation implant. "First her teeth were too white, then her claws weren't long enough, and last time—what was it? Oh yes, the barb on her tail had four spikes instead of five. I'm an artist, not a draftsman."

"But green eyes," Myort protested, albeit in a subdued manner. "The eyes of a Huktra female only turn green when they're carrying a fertilized egg."

"How was I supposed to know that? Keep your wings folded and I'll get a floater scaffold and fix them right now."

"Thanks. I'm taking this Human on board to look over some merchandise."

"You know the rules, Myort. No trading while the ship is in the shop."

"It's only in the shop because you keep getting the details wrong, and this isn't a trade, it's a, uh—"

"Showing," John suggested.

"Right, a showing."

"Hurry up and don't let any of the other customers see you," Wrude grumbled. "You better whistle my praises to your friends for all the grief you've put me through."

The Dollnick stalked off in search of a floater to carry him up to the freighter's nose, and Myort instructed his ship's controller to lower the cargo hatch, which doubled as a ramp. It was steeper than the ramp on John's trader and the helpful claw-holes weren't useful for humans. Myort let out a sigh of exasperation when he noted his companion's lack of progress, and extended his tail.

"Grab a hold, but watch the barb, and don't yank on it or my reflex reaction might throw you across the hold."

John took a quick look around to make sure nobody was watching, and then he grabbed his companion's tail and let the reptile haul him up the ramp into the cargo hold. As soon as they reached level deck, John let go of the tail and was almost knocked over by a gryphon.

"No, Semmi! Down!" Myort barked, but the winged alien lioness with a head like an eagle already had its front paws on the human's shoulders and was licking his face energetically.

"Couldn't you keep a normal cat," John complained, trying to push the gryphon away. "Her tongue is like sandpaper."

"Give her a treat," the Huktra suggested helpfully.

"Yeah, that makes sense, I'll reinforce her bad behavior," John said, but he fished another acorn out of his pocket and offered it to the gryphon. She must have found the gift acceptable because she dropped down on all fours and then tried to stick her beak in John's pocket for more.

"You know what this means," Myort said sadly. "I'm going to have to run a force field to protect those nuts or she'll tear through whatever they're packed in and give herself indigestion."

"Not my problem," John pointed out, still trying to shove the gryphon's head away. "What do you have to show me?"

"So the thing is, I'm heading home from here. My future wife's family owns a chemical business and I thought I'd get a claw in the door with her parents by bringing industrial samples. Lights, please."

The ship's controller brought up the illumination in the hold, and John saw stacks of barrels stenciled with what looked like warnings in more languages than he could count. One yellow drum sported a pictogram of a stick-figure humanoid projectile vomiting, and a black barrel featured a photo-realistic picture of liquid droplets leaving holes in the wings of some flying species.

"You've got to be kidding me, Myort. It looks like you're doing a toxic waste run."

"We have a saying about killing two gryphons with one stone. No, I didn't mean you," the Huktra hastened to add, but it was too late because Semmi was already flying up the companionway to the bridge. "Now she's going to pee on my command chair," Myort said in a resigned voice. "Hey, how about—"

"I never accept alien life forms in trade," John cut him off. "Don't you have anything other than chemicals?"

"I wouldn't have dragged you out here if I didn't think I had something you would want. Those bulk carriers are packed with cyanide salts, and I have plenty of hydrochloric acid."

"You think I want to go into business extracting gold from ore?"

"I heard a rumor you were heading for Borten Four."

"Where do you get your intelligence?"

The Huktra shrugged, basically raising and lowering the tips of his folded wings.

"So maybe I am," John allowed, "but I hate carrying bulk. You know my ship has a fraction of your cargo capacity, plus a quarter of the acorns belong to a friend. I'll need to pay her in cash."

"So how many nuts are we talking?" Myort asked.

"I've got ninety-four standard sacks, the Frunge medium size. I mean, I actually have a hundred and forty-three, but two-thirds of them are half-full."

"This is why I hate dealing with Humans," the Huktra complained, and John's translation implant imparted a long-suffering tone to the alien's words. "Everything with you is a story-problem. Okay, I'll bite. Why are two-thirds of the sacks half full?"

"They belonged to my partner on the job and the full sacks would have been too much for her to carry around. Then she asked me to get rid of them all for her and I didn't bother repacking."

"You know, that's more nuts than I thought you'd have. I saw plenty of them on the ground on Earth, but still..."

"We were days just packing them all," John said. "Would you rather I take a sample back to the bar where I met you and—"

"No, no," Myort cut him off. "Maybe I have some cash after all. You'll take as much cyanide and acid as you're comfortable with and I'll make the rest up somehow. But I'll need some samples from your cargo to make sure the quality is uniform."

By the time John closed the deal with the Huktra and arranged to meet the next day for the exchange, it was already nine in the morning on Universal Human Time, and he hurried to a lift tube to make his other appointment. The security at EarthCent Intelligence waved him past, and he wound a path through the familiar maze of cubicles to Clive Oxford's office.

"Just in time," the director of EarthCent Intelligence greeted John. "I have a meeting with the ambassador, but you can walk with me."

"I should have pinged ahead but I had some business to take care of. By the way, the Huktra I was dealing with knew that I'm on my way to Borten Four."

Clive winced. "We've upgraded our security to Drazen standards, but that hasn't stopped the more advanced species from slipping a bug past us from time to time. I'll have to have my whole office zapped again. Who was it?"

"Myort. Do you know him?"

"He's a handler with Huktra Intelligence, runs all of their field agents in this sector. It's not a big operation because they don't have large populations on any of the Stryx stations."

"Myort told me that if his species has to spend extended time in space, they prefer Zero-G."

"I guess a lot of the winged aliens are like that. Did you make any progress?"

"The money trail on Earth led back to MORE, just like the analysts predicted, but I can't figure out why they're spending so much on discouraging traders from joining the Conference of Sovereign Human Communities. I blew through my bribery budget in just two days to get this much information."

"I'll tell Blythe to make another transfer to your programmable cred," Clive said. "Our business analysts have noticed a sharp increase in foreclosures since the Sharf packaged all of the mortgages they held on human-owned ships as securities and sold them. We've spent some serious time looking into the source of MORE's financing to make sure they aren't backed by some alien group looking for a competitive advantage. It appears that they are raising all of their capital on Earth, which came as a surprise."

"Maybe it's the retirees," John speculated. "Quite a few people who do two full terms as contract workers for one or another of the advanced species end up flush with creds from completion bonuses or balloon payments and decide to buy a retirement place on Earth. MORE sells a number of financial products that guaranty a monthly income, so they probably soak up a lot of retirement savings."

"But there could be criminal funds in there too," Clive said. "When we gave the local governments the information they needed to act against the drug syndicate last year, everybody got a lesson in how cutting off the head doesn't always kill the beast. Selling alien drugs purchased from pirates had pushed aside all sorts of other criminal enterprises because it was just so profitable. The enforcement sweep focused on the leaders and the most violent gang members, but plenty of the lower ranks managed to grab a lot of cash and dodge the police."

"You think that organized crime is getting into financial services?"

"I know that they are, it's not a new thing for them. It's just that breaking up the drug syndicate created a lot of unemployed accountants."

"I suppose it makes sense that they'd look for cleaner work. Do we have a response plan?"

"The problem is that EarthCent doesn't have any financial regulatory power on Earth, that's left to the patchwork of governments the people there live under." Clive approached a set of doors with a blue-and-green globe emblem and they slid open at his approach. "Early," he said, observing that nobody was waiting in the embassy's conference room. He motioned for his companion to enter with him. "Are you going to stand for the council?"

"I still haven't decided," John said. "I've never made a secret of the fact that I'm connected with EarthCent Intelligence, but I doubt many people know that it's my main career and that the trading is just a cover job."

"I'd be surprised if there's an alien intelligence service that doesn't know," Clive said. "It's probably why Myort started doing business with you in the first place."

"Which explains some of the winks he's given me, but I meant other traders. If it came out after I got elected to the council, the conspiracy buffs would have a heyday claiming that I was sent to infiltrate the Traders Guild."

"You could tell them before the election."

"I thought you wanted me to be discrete."

"That made sense when you were a field agent, but since you were promoted to a handler, there's something to be said for going public. Every sentient on the tunnel network knows that if they have intelligence information that may be important for their species, they can go to their embassy and ask for the cultural attaché. But lots of traders have reasons for avoiding the Stryx stations, and those are some of the people we'd be most interested in hearing from. If all the traders knew that you work for us…"

"I'll lose some friends and I may not be welcome in certain places."

"I won't push you, but think about it. Did you go over the Borten Four material?"

"Yes, but other than the capital letters, I don't see the connection with my MORE investigation."

"It started after the Drazens invited the local humans coming off a long-term contract to lease the mining habitat. As soon as the big creds started rolling in, SHARE showed up on the scene and began buying out or leasing asteroid claims. They bring in their own miners on contracts."

"If the claim owners wanted to cash out, what's that to us?"

"That's the way the Drazens see it, and I don't blame them, but according to our information, SHARE has been managing their properties as if the habitat didn't exist. They shuttle in new miners from out-of-system, drop them at the claims, and supply all of their needs."

"I still don't see the problem."

"It's the company store system, John. The miners are dependent on SHARE for not only the food they eat and the water they drink but the very oxygen they breathe. We've obtained copies of the contracts SHARE is offering workers, and while there's nothing illegal about it, you'd never see terms like that in an alien contract."

"The Stryx have standards for interspecies hiring."

"And the aliens have ethics. We have a Verlock co-op student who has been reading up on human history, and he suggested that rather than being an acronym, SHARE is just short for sharecroppers."

"And the crop is gold."

"Nickel, mainly, but gold as well," Clive said. "I want you to see if you can recruit any of those sharecroppers for us so we can figure out what's really going on."

"Could be tricky if they never come in to the habitat. Even in Zero-G, hard rock asteroid mining involves moving a lot of mass around. The miners can probably keep up their muscle tone for a while without sleeping and exercising on the habitat at Earth-normal weight, or whatever they spin the thing at."

"See what you can do, and let me know if you decide to stand for the council. Rendezvous starts in two weeks?"

"I figure I can spend ten days in the Borten system and still make it," John said. He looked around the conference room and nodded in approval. "I like the globe and the table, but I've got to catch some sleep and move a ton of acorns."

Ten

"Are you ready to order?" the waitress asked.

"I think so," Georgia said. She glanced across the small table at Larry, who nodded and waved the holographic menu out of existence. "I'll have the Trader's Special and a small salad."

"What will you have to drink?"

"Is the Frunge tea safe for humans?"

"Everything we serve is safe for human consumption. I've worked here almost a year and I've never seen an alien in the place. I don't think there's been a Frunge on the habitat since they leased it to us."

"Then I'll try it."

The young woman made a note on her tab and turned to Larry.

"I'll have the spaghetti and meatballs and whatever you have on draft," the trader said.

"We're out of draft beer, the only brewer on the habitat had something go wrong with the last batch. We just got in a shipment of red wine from somewhere."

"What kind of red wine?" Georgia asked.

"The red kind," the waitress said, turning back to the reporter. "What other kind could there be?"

"You know, the type of grapes, where it's from, the vintage?"

"You can get red or white, but we're out of the white."

"How about cans?" Larry asked.

"I've never seen wine in cans, though it wouldn't be a bad idea," the waitress mused. "If you want water with a shot of vodka, it gets rid of that yucky recycled taste."

"I'm not really a drinker, just a beer now and then. Do you have any fresh juice?"

"Does it count as fresh if I let you stir in the powder yourself?"

"Close enough," Larry said.

"It will be a few minutes," the waitress told them. "Everything is precooked, but we only have one microwave."

"Too much information," Georgia said to her dinner companion as soon as the waitress was out of earshot. "I'm sorry I dragged you in here. I'm a sucker for décor."

"You mean the tables made from old crates and the netting hanging from the ceiling?"

"It reminds me of a seafood place where I went on a date once while I was in university."

"How was it?"

"The date? A disaster. The food wasn't that great either. I wonder if all the restaurants on Poalim are this bad."

"It's a service habitat for the ice harvesting fleet, Georgia. I'm surprised they grow enough fresh food to even be able to offer a salad. Most places like this have to import all of their food because there's no room for raising crops."

"It didn't look that small when we came in for docking."

"The closer you get to a space structure, the bigger it looks. It's tough to judge the size of these places unless you cheat and ask your ship's controller for help. We're on the commercial deck, and the innermost deck houses the repair facility, but the outer decks are all cabin space."

"Wow, I'd go nuts."

"You're spoiled from living on a Stryx station," Larry said. "People are pretty adaptable, and they come to a habitat like this to make money, not to make a home. Right now this place is sort of a boomtown. Once the easy pickings are gone, most of the population will move on to the next hot ice harvesting play, and the people who remain for the long term will have more space and improve the quality of life here."

"You're kind of a philosopher, do you know that?"

"If I say anything intelligent, it's probably stolen from my dad. The only reason I have a good chance of being elected is because everybody respects him so much."

"Sounds like you're not sure you want the job."

"I do and I don't. The council used to be mainly an honorary thing, their only responsibility was managing the next Rendezvous. There were years my dad had to hunt around on election day sweet-talking friends into running so there would be enough candidates. It's funny, but the main reason he's retiring is because he knows that joining the Conference of Sovereign Human Communities means getting involved in politics."

"You mean CoSHC politics."

"Exactly. The Traders Guild has always been a laid-back organization, and for a lot of the old trader families, Rendezvous is the one time a year they get together to see relatives. But a lot of first-generation traders are expected this year, and they're putting up their own slate of candidates who are against joining CoSHC."

"What do traders have against the Conference of Sovereign Human Communities?"

"It's the whole independence thing. Plenty of traders never sign up with the Guild, even though the dues is just a few creds a year and there aren't any binding laws. If the

114

Guild joins CoSHC, which many think is on its way to becoming the government for humans living away from Earth, that would commit our members to follow their rules."

"Wait a second. You're saying that traders are lawless?"

"We're subject to the laws of whatever jurisdiction we're working in, which usually means alien laws."

"Here's your tea and juice," the waitress said, setting down a tray with a small teapot, a teacup on a saucer, a glass of water, a long-handled spoon, and a small foil packet with a picture of an orange printed on it. "I'll be right back."

"Then we better get cracking," Larry said, tearing open the foil packet and pouring the brownish powder into the water. "Please change colors," he muttered as he stirred the mixture vigorously.

"I think I'll pour off a bit of tea now in case it gets too strong steeping," Georgia said. She removed the teacup and saucer from the tray, and keeping a finger on the teapot lid for safety, poured three-quarters of a cup of the brilliant blue liquid. "This looks interesting."

"I guess this is as orange as it gets," Larry said, setting aside the spoon and taking a sip from his rust-colored drink. "I've had worse."

"Really?"

"Oh, yeah. I could tell you stories that would make you lose your appetite for a week."

Georgia blew on her tea and then tried waving a bit of the steam towards her face to sample the aroma. "It doesn't smell like anything."

"That means it's still good," the waitress said, returning with their meals. "Food smells when it goes bad. That's the first thing they taught me on this job."

"I'm not sure it works that way with tea."

"Tea never goes bad. The owner found a case of old Frunge tea in the storeroom when he rented the place and it hasn't killed anybody yet." The waitress placed a large plate of spaghetti and meatballs in front of Larry and set a sandwich on a plastic dish in front of the reporter. Then she reached in the pocket of her apron and pulled out two forks, giving one to each of her customers. "Will there be anything else?"

"My salad?" Georgia asked.

"You wanted it at the same time as the meal? Everybody on Poalim eats salad for dessert since it's such a treat."

"Whenever you get a chance."

Larry wound some spaghetti onto his fork, stabbed a meatball, and attempted to assume a contemplative expression while chewing. Georgia cautiously lifted the top slice of her sandwich's bread to check how the payload comported with the menu description.

"I'd have to say that they play fast and loose with the ingredients in this place," she said. "If this is a Trader's Special, I'd hate to see a Trader's Regular."

"Don't make me laugh while I'm eating," Larry complained, coughing something into his hand

"How's yours?"

"I've had worse."

"You'll never get a job as a food reporter with that attitude."

"What's wrong with your sandwich?"

"It's missing the avocado, the dill, and the Spanish olives. I'd say what I've got here is a cheese sandwich on white bread."

"That's what the Trader's Special always amounts to. It's traditional to build it up on the menu, sort of an inside joke."

"Here's your salad," the waitress said, putting a bowl of thinly sliced tomatoes with a sprinkling of pepper and some type of oil on top. Bon appétit."

"Am I missing something here?" Georgia asked. "Like, I don't know, lettuce?"

"On Poalim?" The waitress shook her head. "Hydroponic tomatoes are it for fresh veg on this habitat, though somebody told me they're actually considered fruit."

"Good thing I'm not allergic to them."

"Oh, I almost forgot. That's cold-pressed peanut oil and some folks have a problem with it."

"Better late than never," Georgia said. "If you can bring us the check, we're leaving for the Colony One presentation as soon as we're finished and I don't want to be late."

"Remember, it's on me," Larry said. "If you're worried about timing, eat the salad now and take the sandwich with you."

"How about your spaghetti?"

"This? Stop asking me questions and it will be gone in two minutes."

Five minutes later, Larry washed down the last forkful of spaghetti with a swallow of his orange drink, and Georgia gave up any semblance of trying to keep pace. While he went to the register to pay with his programmable cred, she wrapped the remaining half of her sandwich in a napkin.

"It's just down the corridor," Larry told her on his return. "They're holding the presentation in one of the large service bays because it's the only place with enough room."

Somebody had made a real effort to clean up the bay, though they couldn't do much to make the badly scratched deck plates look any better. Colorful bunting was strung along the bulkheads and from the ceiling, and a portable audio/visual system with a holographic projector had been set up on a raised platform at the front of the bay. There were a few folding chairs available for older audience members, but the attendees mainly sat on the floor or stood to the sides.

The audience burst into applause as theme music swelled from the speakers, and Georgia found herself clapping just as enthusiastically as the rest of them. The presenters on stage were all dressed in colorful Colony One uniform tops, which were copied from the same old Earth television show that supplied the music. When the initial round of enthusiasm waned, a grey-haired woman tapped an insignia on her chest that apparently served as a microphone, and just managed to announce, "Space. The fi—" before she was drowned out by the audience shouting the rest of the well-known line.

The reporter found herself tempted to cover her ears with her hands to block out all of the noise that followed. When the cheering and hooting finally ran its course and the presenter launched into her introduction, the lack of subsequent interruptions made Georgia suspect that she had witnessed a clever strategy to let the attendees vent their pent-up emotions so they would calm down and pay attention.

"Welcome to the Colony One traveling roadshow, as we like to call it, and I want to take a moment to clear up any misconceptions," the speaker began. "We are not a cult, the doors are not locked, and we encourage you to use the facilities if nature calls. We won't be accepting any money, so please don't offer. Our mission is to collect contact information and pledges from everybody who is interested in supporting the acquisition and fitting-out of a colony ship capable of sustaining four to six million humans and their livestock in space while searching for a habitable world."

Something like a flash of gold came arcing out of the crowd and hit the stage near the woman. Georgia flinched, wondering if it was an attack. But the presenter just smiled and said, "Please keep your jewelry on as well. This reminds me of the time I was on a Drazen open world and a local human farmer tried to present us with a pair of breeding goats. He had the right idea for colony ship livestock, but in life, as in comedy, timing is everything. Here to speak to you about timing, my colleague, Dollyman."

The audience gave a polite round of applause as a tall man wearing a sports jacket with two extra sleeves sewn across the chest moved to the front of the platform. The new speaker had a tab in his hand, and he used it to activate the holographic projector. A Dollnick colony ship filled the space above the stage, spinning on its axis just as it would to create weight for the inhabitants on a mission.

"I don't have a clue why they call me Dollyman," the presenter began, eliciting a laugh from the attendees, "but I can tell you that I often feel like the luckiest man in the galaxy. A little over thirty years ago I left Earth as a contract worker for a janitorial job that promised good benefits. What nobody had told me was that I would be one of the first humans employed in Prince Drume's orbital shipyards. By the end of my contract, I'd pushed a sonic broom over every square centimeter of a Dollnick colony ship under construction."

The hologram slowly swiveled by ninety degrees, so that most of the audience was now seeing a flat end of the cylindrical vessel. Dollyman continued tapping away on his tab, and layers of the hologram vanished, one after another until all that was left resembled a spoked wheel without a tire.

"What you're looking at is a single section of a Dollnick colony ship without the decks," the presenter continued. "There's no cut-and-dried rule for how many sections a ship can have, though I've been told there's a theoretical limit beyond which the center of gravity begins to create structural complications. The spoke-and-hub design is common to practically all large space structures that host biologicals, including Stryx stations, because a multiple-deck centrifuge is the only practical way to create so-called 'artificial gravity' in space. But my goal here isn't to get into the physics of space construction, which I'm hardly qualified to discuss in any case. Does anybody want to guess how long it takes a Dollnick construction crew to complete a section from this stage?"

"A year," somebody called out.

"A decade," a different voice chipped in.

"Five and a half years," a mathematically oriented person ventured, splitting the difference between the first two guesses to maximize his chances of being closest to the correct answer.

"What if I told you the longest guess was off by more than an order of magnitude?" Dollyman said.

"What's an order of magnitude?" a youngster in the front row asked.

"A factor of ten."

"You mean it takes less than a year?"

"Actually, construction of a single section takes several times a hundred years, and while Dollnicks live longer than that, it's not unusual for a shipyard worker to pass an unfinished construction job along to his son. Of course, an orbital shipyard like Prince Drume's can build a large number of sections at the same time, that's just a question of available workers and materials. The point is, from soup to nuts, building a Dollnick colony ship may take a thousand years."

Georgia heard gasps from the crowd around her, and she had the odd feeling that a good deal of the air had just been sucked from the room. She was recording the presentation audio with her tab, but her fingers tapped away almost mechanically on the virtual keyboard, taking notes about the hologram on display and the scale of the work.

"Disappointed, right?" Dollyman continued. "For those of you who wonder why we aren't talking about building our own colony ship or raising the money to commission aliens to build one for us, there's your answer. Colony ships are one of the milestone achievements of advanced species, and the costs are, if you'll excuse the pun, astronomical. But, there is another option, the one we're here to talk to you about today. Sally?"

The grey-haired woman returned to the front of the stage. Dollyman passed her the tab and then stood to the side. Sally swiped at the screen, and the hologram of the Dollnick colony ship section was replaced by a somewhat smaller cylindrical vessel that looked like it had been through the wars.

"This is the Chorp, a Class B Drazen colony ship that was recently towed into a Sharf recycling orbital for scrapping. The jump drive is a pile of slag, the environmental systems have been shut down for hundreds of

121

years, and at some point the asteroid deflection system was scavenged for another vessel, leading to multiple impacts. Before you ask, we aren't bidding on the Chorp. The reason I'm showing you this hologram is that I've seen the Drazen estimate for restoring this ship to liveable condition, and it came to a half a trillion creds."

This time the audience groaned, but the presenter continued relentlessly.

"That's right. If one in twenty humans alive today coughed up a thousand creds each, humanity could be the proud owner of an empty Drazen colony ship capable of moving approximately two million of us to a new home."

"So what are we doing here?" a new voice cried out in disgust.

"I'm glad you asked that question," Sally said. "The purpose of the Colony One movement is to make humanity aware of the sacrifices required to become a true spacefaring species, sacrifices we were never called on to make because of our early admission to the tunnel network. That's the tough-love part of our presentation, but now let me show you what awaits us, or rather our grandchildren, if we back our words with deeds."

The rest of the presentation, large parts of which were licensed from Grenouthian documentary producers, took the audience through the range of missions colony ships were capable of performing. Georgia had always thought that these giant vessels were basically moveable space farms that provided a temporary home to emigrants, but it turned out that they were worlds in miniature, intended to preserve a full civilization.

"What happens if after generations in space, the best world a colony ship finds is already occupied?" somebody asked during one of the breaks for questions.

"If the colony ship belongs to a tunnel network species, they would be bound by Stryx rules," Colony One's legal expert replied. "Before you ask, the number of possible scenarios is mind-boggling, but in all cases, the first step is to contact the Stryx, who would send a science ship to evaluate the situation."

"What if the colony ship wasn't sent by a tunnel network species?"

"You don't want to know."

Eleven

"Morning," Marshall greeted Ellen. "Nice to have you back."

"I'm surprised you're still here," she said, spreading her blanket next to his. "I've been all over the planet the last couple weeks, but I thought you'd had enough of Earth for the time being."

"I left the day after we met and I returned this morning," he said, rising to help her unload the rented floater, which was piled high with goods from her ship. "I did a Moon run and then decided to come back until I leave the system for Rendezvous."

"I've never been to the Moon. What's it like for trade?"

Marshall shrugged. "A little of this, a little of that. About the same as what you'd see at any moon colony. My older brother leases a crater there that he's turned into a greenhouse. His wife is a botanist and it's sort of their retirement dream."

"You mean a crater, as in—" Ellen spread her hands as if she were describing the fish that got away.

"Not that big," he replied with a laugh, and returned to the floater for another load. "What did your proprietary trading platform suggest to you this time?"

"They're still pushing disposable stunners and tablecloths," she said in disgust. "I decided to bring everything they recommended over the last three months to clean house before Rendezvous."

"Fire sale?"

"Pretty much. I've got enough data for the piece I'm writing. Now I just need to round it out by getting some interviews with other traders who have used the Advantage platform. I'll do that at Rendezvous."

"Did you get any trading done in the last two weeks?"

"The truth is I was too busy meeting with journalists. It looks like the replacement news syndicate I was telling you about is going to become a reality."

"Does that mean you're in line for a promotion?" Marshall asked, helping her set out an array of Horten art glass.

"I messaged my boss I wasn't ready to give up the trader's life to become a full-time editor, so the paper made up a new job title for me. Meet the new Earth Syndication Coordinator."

"What does it mean?"

"I'm on the hook to return here once a month for the next year and meet with correspondents about projects they want to sell us. By pre-buying stories from investigative journalists, the Galactic Free Press will have some control over the syndication feed, rather than just taking whatever comes up. It's sort of like middle-management, I guess, but at least I have the rest of the month to myself."

"Smart of your boss," Marshall observed. "If they had hired somebody from Earth, it would have meant an office and hiring support staff."

"You were in the business?" Ellen asked. She dismissed the rented floater and started unpacking all of the smaller items she'd brought.

"Not the newspaper business, the distribution business. And it was a long time ago, but my memory is that one manager leads to another, and before you know it, you have a whole office of people making work for each other."

"Excuse me," an athletic-looking man in his forties interrupted them. "Is that a genuine paddle-cup-mitt-ball set?"

"Yes, sir," Marshall said, returning to his own blanket and picking up the boxed set to better display it to the customer. "It's competition-grade, never used, and you can see Prince Gruer's seal on the flap."

"I've been looking for one of these since I moved back to Earth, but all I've found are cheap knock-offs."

"I took this one in trade at the elevator hub on Jufe Two, an ag world in the—"

"I worked there for twenty years," the man cut off the explanation. "Sometimes I'm not sure why I ever left. May I?" The trader handed over the bulky package and the customer inspected the seal and nodded. "How much?"

"Let's call it an even hundred."

"I shouldn't have told you how long I've been looking for one of these," the man grumbled, but he held out a programmable cred. "A competition set didn't cost forty creds back on Jufe."

The trader slotted the coin into his mini-register and frowned. "You're short."

"I thought it would save time haggling. Can you do eighty-seven? That's our team's programmable cred and my wife will kill me if I add my own money."

Marshall grimaced as he keyed in the transaction, and the customer gave his voice confirmation.

"Thanks," the ex-ag worker said. "At least you know the set is going to a good home."

After the customer moved off with his prize, Ellen asked, "How did you know there would be any demand for a paddle-cup-mitt-ball set on Earth? You need four arms to play."

"The leagues on Earth just double the number of players per position, but I've seen humans on Dollnick open worlds wearing prosthetic arm sets," Marshall replied. "I had the feeling that I could get the best price for the set on Earth because there's not enough demand here for anybody to have started importing them. Sporting equipment is a low-risk proposition in most cases, and if there's an official seal, it's as good as cash."

"Before I started using the Advantage platform, I specialized in craft goods," Ellen told him, casting a mournful look at the commodity merchandise spread around her blanket. "Some of the art supplies barely weigh anything, and if I spread enough sparkles on the blanket, children would drag their parents over and I could make a killing on crayons and stickers. I did really well with sewing supplies too, especially the alien gear."

"And then you decided to throw away your money and time trying to chase the crowds?"

"It's for a story. I can afford to experiment more than most traders with a mortgage because the Galactic Free Press is pretty generous with freelancers. I just wish I could come up with a name for what the Advantage platform is promoting. Follow the leader? Me-too mercantilism?"

"Cash-crop syndrome," her neighbor suggested, redistributing the remaining merchandise on his own blanket to cover the bare spot left by the paddle-cup-mitt-ball set. "The older traders I know, every cred we earned that didn't go into feeding ourselves or paying customs bribes went to the ship's mortgage. We counted our wealth in goods, not coins, and the whole 'barter is better' thing wasn't just a tunnel network slogan for us, it was a way of life. But somebody starts offering young traders easy credit and it turns into a race for cash."

"Did you just make that up, or is it a real syndrome?" Ellen asked. "I've never heard of it before."

"It's not a medical condition if that's what you mean, but cash-crop farming started not far from here a few hundred years ago. Joint-stock companies started pooling capital to build canals, which were soon replaced by railroads, and the next thing you knew, family farms that hadn't ever been in debt were all working for the bank."

"Because they had to pay for the railroads?"

"The railroads changed the whole business model of farming. Instead of feeding the family and raising some extra livestock for cash to pay for luxuries, farmers turned to monoculture and started planting whatever they thought would maximize the income from their land. You had whole regions growing just a couple of crops, or specializing in pigs and chickens because the railroads made it possible to reach the big cities. But efficiency has its price, and farmers who put all of their eggs in one basket could be wiped out by a drought, a disease, or worse, by a bumper crop depressing the price for the one product they had to sell."

"Kind of like traders following the advice from Advantage and showing up on some planet with the same goods as everybody else. Are you from a farm family?"

"Read a few books about it in Zero-G," Marshall said with a grin. "Family farms are actually making a comeback on Earth now. The alien exporters don't like buying from factory farms, and they're not as obsessed with scaling up single product lines as our own exporters. Say 'Drazen Foods' and everybody thinks hot peppers, but they actually try to sell every Earth ingredient in the All Species Cookbook."

"How much for one of those tablecloths?" a woman asked, pointing at the small pile Ellen had set out without much hope.

"What's the best price you've seen today?"

"Forty-two," the woman replied. "There's a trader—"

"Forty if you buy right now. I'm not interested in getting caught in a bidding war," Ellen said gruffly.

"How about quantity three?"

"Are you a retailer?"

"I've got a mother and a sister. If I had a retail shop, I would have asked the price for the whole stack."

"How about one ten?" Ellen offered.

"All I've got is a hundred."

"Cash?"

The woman produced a hundred-cred coin.

"I've got to check this," Ellen said, and slotted the coin in the mini-register just to make sure it wasn't counterfeit. "All right. Pick out three."

"You really are liquidating," Marshall said after the customer left with her tablecloths. "I'm sure you could at least have gotten your money back anywhere else in the galaxy."

"And here I'm selling at fifteen creds under my cost, each," she acknowledged. "But I got a bonus from the Galactic Free Press that covered my losses, and the Syndication Coordinator gig will keep me healthy going forward. Reporting that I actually sold at a loss will help make the point in my story, and besides, I don't really know anything about tablecloths or art glass."

"If you put it that way, I suppose there's a certain logic to making a clean start," Marshall said. "Will you go back to crafting goods?"

"I can hardly wait," Ellen replied with a grin. "Hey, do you see anything you want?" she asked, gesturing at the goods on her blanket. "I know you'd rather barter than buy, but it's hard to beat below cost."

"I went to a bankruptcy auction not long ago and it made me feel like a vulture picking over a corpse. In the end, the only thing I bought was a meal for the trader who had been foreclosed."

"I've heard of traders quitting the business but never a bankruptcy auction. Do you mean the Sharf repossessed and sold everything on board?"

"Not the Sharf, the trader had refinanced with some Earth company. I've known plenty of traders over the years who gave up and sold out, but there's always a demand for the ships. The Sharf never cared who took over the payments as long as the mortgage got paid. The trader whose stuff was being auctioned said she had friends interested in buying her ship, but the mortgage holder insisted on getting the missed payments and penalties upfront. There were also a bunch of would-be traders at the auction waiting to bid on the ship, but in the end, the auctioneer announced a reserve bid that was way over the value and that was it."

"I don't understand. You're saying that they only sold the trader's inventory and not the ship?"

"Right."

"But the mortgage was on the ship, not her inventory!"

"That's what you'd think, but apparently the refi deal was secured by all of the borrower's personal assets, not just the ship. Right after the meal, Bethany, that was the

130

trader's name, headed for the local labor exchange to sign up for an alien contract to restore her finances. She said she'd had enough of dealing with her own people."

"You know what? I should make that my next story. I know that the Sharf sold my mortgage to some Earth outfit because that's when I found out about Advantage, but I didn't think I had a reason to care who held the note on the ship."

"I might have heard a rumor that EarthCent Intelligence is already looking into it."

"Yeah, but they don't have any agents on Earth."

"Ah, the noninterference deal that EarthCent made with the governments here. I hadn't thought of that."

"So you're not with them?"

"EarthCent Intelligence?" Marshall rubbed his nose and laughed. "They've only been around for two decades at the most, and I'll need more of a history than that before I go pledging my loyalty. I know plenty of traders who dabble in it, though, so if you need a contact..."

"Thanks, but I've got a good friend who's in deep with them, even though he pretends it's only a sideline. I just wondered because you're traveling alone and you're much friendlier than most solo traders your age I've met."

"It's not an easy life, and a lot of my generation saw it as a zero-sum game, where more traders meant less business. Some of the old hands blame young traders for everything from high wholesale costs to low retail prices, but I see it the opposite way."

"You think that new traders lower wholesale costs and raise retail pricing?"

"I mean that trade isn't a zero-sum game. The more of us there are, the more marketplaces become available. If you gave me a choice between rolling out the blanket somewhere with no other traders within a light-year or participating in an active fair like this one, I'll take your company every time. It's much easier to draw customers when there are a bunch of us together."

"But every great trading story I know involves visiting some isolated population that has valuable trade goods they're willing to barter for common merchandise they can't get otherwise," Ellen protested.

"I've been in this business longer than you've been alive and it's never happened for me or anybody I've known well enough to trust. Think about it. The Sharf two-man traders most of us fly can't jump on their own, they need tunnel access to cover interstellar distances. The Stryx don't open tunnels to sparsely occupied systems, so the only way a trader is likely to encounter an isolated population is on some neglected moon or a large mining asteroid."

"But a few weeks ago I set down in a town not that far north of here that was only occupied by deer and coyotes."

"Going into the acorn trade?" Marshall asked with a wink.

"You know about the Huktra?"

"I saw something about the Traders Guild adding acorns to the export commodities list while I was catching up with the news on my way back from the Moon."

"My friend was right about trade secrets being the most fleeting of all," she said. "I wonder how much he got for my share."

"Timing is everything. The article in the trader's section of the Galactic Free Press showed a graph for the acorn futures price that was only a week old and it looked like a downhill ski slope. I'm surprised you didn't see it."

"I haven't been reading the trader's section lately," Ellen admitted. "I know, it's stupid of me, but I've been concentrating on Earth news because of the new job, and the Advantage platform has private discussion groups for trade news where people really let their hair down."

"You have a buzz cut," Marshall pointed out.

"Yeah. The truth is, the people on those discussion groups were mainly interested in politics, why traders should vote against joining the Conference of Sovereign Human Communities and all that. I mainly stuck with the hot-markets thread, but I don't have the time to spend on chasing rainbows. I suppose it's good to know there are still opportunities out there for traders who are light on their feet, but you'd have to spend half of your life in Stryx tunnels to make use of the information."

"Did it ever occur to you they might be doing it on purpose? Maybe some of your generation sees trade as a zero-sum game too, and they're trying to winnow out the competition by sending them on wild-goose chases."

"You think that the high-reputation posters in the Advantage group are lying in order to trick the rest of us into losing money?" Ellen frowned. "I can't believe what an idiot I am. Here I've been thinking that it's just a really bad platform, but now you've got me wondering if that's on purpose."

"Don't be so hard on yourself. Taking advantage of one's reputation in a closed community is one of the oldest tricks in the book. It's a type of affinity scheme. And it looks to me like you've got a fish on the hook."

"What?" Ellen looked around and saw a teenager crouched on his heels, his eyes fixed on one of her more expensive mistakes.

"Can I try one of those fishing reels?" he asked her. "They look a little different from what I use."

"They're the basic type sold on Vergallian tech-ban worlds," she told him, handing over one of the spinning reels. "It's saltwater safe, ball bearing construction, and you can see that the hand is reversible just by flipping the crank mechanism to the other side."

"What's the recovery?"

"You mean how much line comes back in a single crank? I don't remember the conversion from Vergallian units, but it's the standard amount."

"So you don't know the maximum drag either?"

"Do you see the indicator on the side?"

"You mean I have to set the drag manually?" the teen asked, looking disappointed.

"Vergallian reels are all equipped with a fractional drag selector. The default setting is twenty-five percent of the breaking strength."

"So I have to do an alien unit conversion and enter the test strength somewhere?" He turned the reel over again to see if he had missed something.

"That's the blue button on the side. When you change the fishing line, press it, and the reel automatically tests the breaking strength of the line."

"Are you serious? That's so cool, but now I know I can't afford it."

"Twenty-five creds?" Ellen suggested.

"Really? Deal," the teenager said. He pulled out a change purse and began to count out five-cred pieces. "If this thing works like you say, all of my friends are going to want one. Hey, how much for the carton?"

"All sixteen? That would be four-hundred creds."

"No discount?"

134

"I quoted you my cost. I'm sort of cleaning house."

"Hold on," the teen said, and pulled out his phone. A few seconds later, he continued out loud. "Dad? I was on my way to see you and I stopped in the—yeah, I know, but there's a trader with Vergallian fishing reels for twenty-five creds and—he'll be here in a minute," the kid concluded, putting the phone back in his pocket. "Dad works at the ground station for the elevator and he's a bit nuts about fishing. If the reels are everything you say they are, we'll take them all."

Twelve

"Welcome to the Borten Habitat," a scruffy looking young man called up to John before the ramp even touched the deck of the landing bay. "Got any work for a cash-poor trader?"

"Talk to me," John replied without hesitation. "I'm not a charity, but maybe you have some information I can use." The ramp reached the deck, but rather than starting down, he gestured to the young man to come on board. "You hungry?"

"I could eat Vergallian vegan."

"That bad, huh? I'm John."

"Mario," the young man identified himself. "Just so you know, I won't be able to invite you over in return because I lost my ship."

"Pirates?" John asked, leading his unexpected guest to the ladder.

"Bankers," Mario replied. "I did a cash-out refi six months ago but I couldn't keep up with the payments. They tried to point me in the direction of some good business but nothing seemed to work."

"MORE?"

"That's them. But don't get me wrong, it's a great company. They even offered to let me keep living on the ship to fly consignments for some package network they're setting

136

up, but I just couldn't see doing that after being my own boss."

"Leftover pizza all right with you?" John offered. "I ordered it from the takeout place when I got in so it's less than eight hours old."

"Pizza's great. So you've already taken care of your business here? I was hoping I could make myself useful."

"Delivered some ore, ate a few slices, and fell asleep. I'm one of those weirdos who gets bone-tired whenever I go from Zero-G to getting some weight back, even if it's just on a habitat." He removed two slices of pizza from the box, put them on a plate for the microwave, and instructed the ship controller, "Thirty seconds."

"I've been all over this place looking for work," Mario said, unable to keep his eyes off the rotating plate visible through the microwave's tinted door as he spoke. "You mentioned a delivery. Are you in the consignment business?"

"That was just dropping off some ore for a friend. My cargo includes some good chemicals for extracting gold — cyanide salts and hydrochloric acid. I'm sure I could sell them to the cooperative that runs the refining center here on the habitat, but I think I could get a better price from independent operators."

"Ding," the ship's controller announced, and John removed the plate and handed it to his guest.

"Half and half?" Mario asked, taking a slice and offering the plate to his host.

"I've already hit my pizza quota for the day. Take your time and eat, there's more in the box if you want, and there's plenty of water. I actually have somebody coming to meet me so I've got to head back down."

137

"I'll come with you," the hungry guest offered through a mouthful of pizza. "You can't be comfortable leaving a stranger on your bridge."

"I've got the security upgrade for my ship controller," John told him bluntly. "It will inform me if you start poking around. Just relax and get some food in and then we'll talk."

Fifteen minutes later, when Mario went looking for his host, he found John engaged in close conversation with a familiar-looking young woman who was dressed in black. He was about to head back up to the bridge to let them conduct their business in private when John motioned him over.

"Mario, this is Sharon. I mentioned your situation to her and she said she knew about you."

"I'm the third shift bartender at Green Earth," the woman explained, naming the most popular bar on the habitat. "You told me your life story a couple of times while you drank your last ten creds."

"Sorry about that," the bankrupt trader said. "I must have gotten pretty drunk not to recognize you right away. I hope I had enough left for a tip."

"It's probably better you don't remember," Sharon said. "I've got to get going. Good luck, Mario. John helped me out of a jam one time, so listen to him."

"Thanks," Mario said, and turned to his benefactor. "All fed and reporting for work, Boss."

"Sharon told me there's a new claim consolidator working the asteroid belt. The independent operators I was hoping to sell my chemicals to don't come in to the habitat anymore."

"You're talking about SHARE. The miners who held onto their claims aren't very happy about it. I pick up a day or two of work here and there going out with solo prospectors to help load ore. They say that SHARE hires people who don't have any regard for the basic rules of asteroid mining. It gets more and more hazardous commuting to claims every day with all the blasting going on."

"Then I guess we'll have to hit the asteroid belt to look for customers. Do you have any things you need to get?"

"All I have are the clothes on my back. I thought about going to work for SHARE myself, but then I decided to try to hold out until I could work my passage to the elevator hub on Borten Four. I'm sure the Drazens would give me a short term contract so I could earn enough for a ticket to a Stryx station."

"Play it straight with me and I'll take you to Rendezvous. It's at Aarden this year, the Vergallian Fleet open world that was recently admitted to the tunnel network. The EarthCent circuit ship is making her first stop there at the same time, and Flower always has work for humans."

"I'll play it so straight that you could use me to draw lines. But I thought those Fleet Vergallians broke away from their empire because they didn't want to be tunnel network members."

"And they're not, but there are so many humans living on Aarden that the Stryx opened a tunnel based on our population and economic activity there."

"So what do you want me to do?" Mario asked.

"I've only been in the Borten system once, and I never made it to the asteroid belt, so you can be my guide. Do you think you can locate any of the claims managed by SHARE?"

"Piece of cake. All we have to do is watch for an expanding debris field and then backtrack it to the source."

"Makes sense." John punched the button next to the ramp, watched while it closed, and then led the way back up to the bridge. "You cleaned up after yourself."

"I kind of finished off the pizza," Mario said guiltily.

"You did me a favor. Strap into the co-pilot seat. Controller. Recognize Mario as a guest."

"Please state your name for voice recognition," the controller responded.

"Mario."

"Now you won't be stranded if I eat the cyanide and fall into the hydrochloric acid," John told him. "Controller. Negotiate departure with the habitat's traffic control and let me know when they release us. Main viewer on."

The ship began to move almost immediately, and Mario commented, "That was quick."

"The Drazens source their habitat landing systems from the Dollnicks. When you go to the expense of building a structure this big, there's no point trying to save a few creds on the manipulator fields for traffic control that keep visitors from crashing into it," John pointed out.

"I always hated instructing my controller to hand over control to the local traffic system."

"Nobody likes it, but I can't think of a better alternative. So, do you mind if I ask you about losing your ship? I know repossessions are becoming more common, but I haven't ever seen one taking place."

"You haven't missed anything exciting," Mario said. "They came for my ship less than twenty-four hours after the final deadline for my missed payment passed. I'd been trying to sell my goods for any cash I could get, but it turned out that a dozen or so traders beat me to the punch. By the time I laid out my blanket here, everybody within a light-year had enough canned fish to last them a lifetime."

"What else did you bring?"

"Canned beans, Boston brown bread, canned vegetables—I mean, who ever heard of asteroid miners having too much canned food on hand? Nobody was willing to pay cash, and by that point, there was no sense bartering because the only way I could make the payment on time was through my mini-register."

"You didn't bring any prospecting supplies at all?"

"That's what people kept asking me, but I checked Advantage before I came, and canned food took up the top ten slots on the hotlist. My previous stop was at Void station, so I had no trouble trading everything else I had left there to go all-in on cans. The ironic thing is that within a day of my ship being repossessed with all of my merchandise, I would have killed for a case of beef stew."

"I hope you don't mean that literally," John said.

"No, but I had some hungry days."

"And you said the repo team was nice about it?"

"Yeah, they were actually the same reps who helped me with the refi. They both felt terrible about having to take my ship, but that's part of their job. The woman piloted the ship they came on and the guy followed her in my ship."

"How did they get here so fast? It takes at least a day to travel to the habitat from the tunnel at top speed."

"I asked them about that and they said they happened to be in the system already to meet with other clients. I guess when a mortgage goes delinquent, MORE assigns the repossession to the nearest team, and I just got unlucky. Sometimes I think my luck ran out back when the Sharf sold my mortgage, because I was doing okay before then. Not getting rich, but I made my payments and I wasn't starving."

"Traffic control has released navigation lockout," the ship's controller reported.

"Run a filter on the nearest part of the asteroid belt to check for debris from explosions," John instructed. "Report when you find—"

"There are signs of recent explosions throughout the target volume of space."

"Put the closest one on the main viewer. Recognize anything, Mario?"

"Yeah, that's exactly what the miners were complaining about. That big asteroid that looks sort of like a dumbbell has a half-dozen claims staked on it, and I did some work for two of the prospectors there. It's getting pelted with micro-debris right now, and I'll bet the miners who set off the charge on that egg-shaped rock not far off never even transmitted a fire-in-the-hole warning."

"I'm surprised the others don't get together and run them off."

"The way I heard it, SHARE sort of snuck up on everybody," Mario said. "They sent some advance agents to quietly buy up claims, and then they brought in a transport with a couple thousand contract miners in one go. They're bringing in new miners and supplies and taking out the ingots at least once a week."

"But they don't process the ore at the local habitat."

"Nope. That's one of the reasons I had such a hard time making ends meet—there's not enough work left. SHARE brought in an old Frunge mining ship that handles crushing the ore and separating the metals, nobody knows if it's leased or owned. And the guys running it just eject the waste back into the asteroid belt. It's a complete mess."

"Any idea where that ship is stationed?"

"They move it around, almost like they're trying to spread rock dust over as much space as possible just to make life hard on the independents. I don't know if your controller—"

"Frunge mining vessel Gzelda located," the ship's controller interrupted. "Shall I intercept?"

"Yes, and try to raise them on the comms," John replied.

"Hey, that's not a standard ship controller," Mario said. "It sounds almost like AI."

"In addition to the security add-on for the basic tunnel navigation controller licensed from the Stryx, I have expert system software for solo operations. It's what people back on Earth would have called artificial intelligence before we found out that to everybody else in the galaxy, AI implies non-biological sentience."

"Does it give you trading advice? I could have used something like that."

"Gzelda responded to my hail with a warning to keep our distance or they won't be responsible for our safety," the controller announced.

"Tell them I've got gold extraction chemicals for—tell them it's salvage I'm looking to unload for cash," John interrupted himself. "And ask for a comm channel again. Promise I'll make it worth their while."

"Hey, boss," Mario said. "I'm not one to call the kettle black, but when you say 'salvage', do you mean you've been dealing with the Free Republic?"

"No, I got the goods in barter from a Huktra, but I've found that crooked people are more likely to buy if they think that you're one of them. Controller, divert more power to the dust shields. I don't like the look of this space we're getting into."

"Already done," the ship's controller replied. "I have a positive response from Gzelda. Opening comms."

A dour woman in her fifties whose face looked a bit puffy from too much time spent in Zero-G appeared on the main viewer. Her eyes flicked past Mario, dismissing him, and settled on John. "Make it quick," she said.

"I've got a load of cyanide salts and hydrochloric acid and the habitat processor says they've got all they need," John said. "I'm on my way to Rendezvous and Vergallian customs has a whole thing with hazardous chemical control forms I'd just as soon avoid."

The woman snorted and looked off to her right, obviously getting information from somebody who was invisible to the camera. "You have to identify yourself as a reporter when I ask if you're with the Galactic Free Press, and I'm asking."

"Not me," John said and laughed. "It would make me very unhappy should word of our business get around."

The woman stared out of the viewscreen at him for almost a half a minute before making up her mind. "We'll divert the waste ejection for thirty seconds when you approach, but longer than that, you're going to get the paint sand-blasted off your pretty ship. Our bay can fit four ships your size, and there's only one in there at the moment, so you shouldn't have any trouble landing. If your approach looks wrong to our factory controller, it will blast you with the primary asteroid defense system, so don't screw around."

"Got it," John said. "Estimated time of arrival—"

"Thirty-seven minutes," the ship's controller put in.

The viewscreen went back to showing the asteroid belt, but both men were pressed into their seats as the ship accelerated. Despite the fact that asteroid belts throughout

144

the galaxy were famed for being mainly space and very little asteroid, the ship had to perform multiple course corrections to avoid debris on the way to the Gzelda, leaving neither man in the mood for chitchat. Thirty-seven minutes and eighteen seconds later, the two-man Sharf trader decelerated hard as the simple momentum scavenging field favored by Frunge shipbuilders brought it to rest in the docking bay.

"Factory ships always look beat up, but this one must be around a million years old," John commented on the image presented by the main viewscreen as he unbuckled his safety restraints.

"Don't radiation and metal fatigue cut that short?" Mario asked.

"I wasn't being literal, but the Frunge are advanced enough to have workarounds, though nothing as reliable as Stryx stasis fields." He activated his magnetic cleats and swung around in the chair to bring his boots into contact with the deck. Then he shuffled to a locker, palmed it open, and removed a belt with a holstered Dollnick stunner. "Listen," John said. "I don't expect trouble here, but if anything does happen, just tell them the truth about hitching a ride."

"I'm not a hero, but I'll take one of those if you've got a spare," the young man offered. "I had one on my ship but I didn't get a chance to grab it. The repossession happened so quickly."

John shot an appraising look at his passenger, and then removed another belt from the locker and pushed it gently across the cabin in Zero-G. Mario caught it, fastened the belt, and checked the charge on the power pack. There was a loud banging from below, and rather than making their

145

hosts wait, John ordered the controller to lower the ramp as he headed for the ladder.

The woman who had answered the comms was accompanied by three muscle-bound thugs who didn't look like they knew anything about running a metallurgical factory ship. They were halfway up the ramp by the time John and Mario were in position to meet them.

"Where is it?" she demanded.

"Controller, work lighting," John instructed. "All of those drums behind the netting are hydrochloric acid, and the stackable containers with the skull and crossbones are the cyanide."

"Nice artwork," the woman said grudgingly. "Do it yourself?"

"I have a stencil," John admitted. "I'll trade you for straight weight in nickel ingots unless you'd rather pay in gold."

The oldest joke in space drew a short bark of laughter from the leader and smirks from her three musclemen, decreasing the tension in the hold by several degrees.

"Ten ingots for the lot and you don't have to fill out any forms," she countered.

"Fifteen, and five minutes of your time," John said. "I've got a good source for this stuff and I'm trying to build a steady customer base who can take quantity."

"My time is worth more than that," the woman said. "Ten ingots and I'll join you on your bridge while these four make the exchange."

"Fair enough. Mario, make sure you load an ingot for every two drums and three containers that goes out."

"Got it, boss," the young man said.

The woman nodded for John to precede her up the ladder, leaving the four younger men to work the transfer.

Once they reached the bridge, she looked around, and spotting the manual override to close the hatch, hit it. "A little privacy," she said.

"We may be on my ship, but we're inside your ship," John pointed out.

"I'm just a hired gun who knows how to run the equipment because I worked a twenty-year contract for the Frunge, but as a technician, not a captain," she said. "I committed to six months here to get the operation up and running for SHARE, and believe you me, I won't be signing an extension. My name's Liz," she added, looking him straight in the eyes. "Liz Barnes, and I run the operation the way they tell me. You happened to come on a day that my minder is off giving somebody else a hard time or we wouldn't be having this conversation."

"But you're authorized to trade..."

"Those ten ingots wouldn't pay for twenty percent of what you're giving me and you know it. You're some kind of cop, aren't you? Are you working for the Frunge? The Drazens? I was in a bad situation when I took this deal and I had no way of knowing how SHARE operated." She reached in her coverall's pocket and pulled out a data chip that might have been for a home entertainment system. "Names, dates, documents. I've been hoping somebody like you would come along and I want to make a deal."

"You're only half right," John said. "I'm with EarthCent Intelligence. We work closely with the Drazens and ISPOA but I'm here on our own operation."

"What's ISPOA?"

"The Inter Species Police Operations Agency. Why do you think the Frunge would be closing in? Is this ship stolen?"

"The Gzelda? If she's stolen then there's a scrapyard owner somewhere wondering what happened to one of his piles of junk. No, I heard that SHARE is planning to expand to Break Rock, and the habitat there is still owned by the Frunge, even though everything is leased to humans. Something tells me that my former employers won't be as tolerant as the Drazens when it comes to an operation like SHARE depreciating their assets."

John hesitated, and then pulled an odd-looking ring off his finger. "Okay, here's what I can do. The only way I can shield you if ISPOA gets involved is if you're working for us. That's a Drazen poison detection ring, standard issue for our field agents, so if you get caught up in a sweep, it should convince the Frunge to check your story with us. Your name goes on the rolls as an undercover source, and any EarthCent cultural attaché will be able to vouch for you. Good enough?"

Liz pushed the data chip towards John and he sent the ring back the same way. The two objects passed each other in flat Zero-G trajectories and were caught by their respective targets. "Deal," the woman said.

They both headed back to the hatch and pulled themselves down the ladder to the cargo deck. The swap was already wrapping up, so the musclemen must have been good for something after all. Mario called to John from the area where the chemicals had been stacked. "You better have a look at this, Captain."

John shuffled over on his magnetic cleats, bracing himself to see metal eaten away by a hydrochloric acid leak. His temporary guest was pointing at a large container that the EarthCent Intelligence agent didn't recognize.

"Are they dumping their trash on us or something?"

"No," Mario said. "It was behind the drums and containers you just traded for ingots. The thing is," the young man hesitated, "I think I heard something moving inside. The container has holes in it."

"Controller, close the main hatch," John ordered, suddenly feeling very tired. "Mario, you better go up on the bridge and lock yourself in, just in case."

"I'm not afraid of a couple of space rats."

"If it is what I think it is, it eats space rats for snacks."

"There's something taped to the side," Mario offered helpfully. "Maybe a packing slip?"

John shuffled forward, hoping against hope that his intuition had failed him, and pulled the folded note off the container. The hand-printed scrawl read:

John,

I hope you don't mind babysitting Semmi for a few weeks. She'll probably sleep through most of it since I've had her up for months. I'll catch up to you at Rendezvous and make it worth your while.

Myort

Thirteen

"Have you been to Aarden before?" Georgia asked Larry. Her fingers dug into the armrests of the co-pilot's chair as the two-man trader barreled through the atmosphere, its direct energy conversion shield shedding excess heat as electrical discharges. "It will be weird for me walking on a real planet after living on Union Station for three years."

"It's my first time here," Larry replied, his eyes on the main viewscreen as the ship broke through a concentration of thunder clouds, adding its own lightning to the show. "The Stryx opened the tunnel just recently. Didn't you say you worked on the All Species Cookbook?"

"Tasting recipes, but what does that have to do with it?"

"You know that Aarden is a Fleet Vergallian world and they never signed the tunnel network treaty. There's a rumor that the real reason the Stryx agreed to connect the planet has to do with some multi-party negotiation in which the Imperial Vergallians agreed to stop trying to undermine EarthCent. Supposedly the cookbook was at the center of the deal."

"Oh, that. The word in the newsroom was that there were a bunch of secret treaties involved, and unfortunately, the aliens are better at keeping their mouths shut than we are. Besides, I thought that the sovereign human community on Aarden was one of the biggest, and they were enough to meet the requirement for a tunnel exit without the Vergallians."

"Close to thirty million of us at last count," Larry confirmed. "There are a couple of Dollnick open worlds with more humans than Aarden, and maybe the Drazens and the Frunge each have a planet that comes close, but it is a lot of people to be living on an alien world without being there as contract workers. Like I said, the cookbook thing was just a rumor I heard."

"Are you sure I'll have time to take the elevator up to orbit and find transportation to Flower before the Colony One ship arrives?"

"Easily. You'll be able to spend a full day on the ground helping me prepare for the election before you have to leave, but I thought you were giving up on that story."

"I hope to at least get an article about Flower's open house out of it. The Colony One people said they've arranged tours for whoever shows up, and I also have a friend on board. Dianne used to cover the entertainment scene on Union Station for the Galactic Free Press and she helped me get started on restaurant reviews."

"Touchdown in sixty seconds," the ship's controller announced. "Deceleration at two G's."

The pair saved their breath as their weight increased to double of what it would have been on Earth, and one minute later the Sharf trade ship set down on its shock-absorbing landing gear with barely a bump. The image on the main viewscreen was replaced with a silver-haired woman whose face was split by a wide smile.

"Mom," Larry said. "You got here before us."

"I've been tracking your transponder since you came out of the tunnel, but your father told me not to interrupt during the approach and landing. You're right next to us."

"I gave the controller the coordinates for the campsite Dad sent, so complain to him if you didn't want me for a neighbor."

"And who's your friend?"

"Mom, this is Georgia Hunt. Georgia, Mom."

"Pleased to meet you, Mrs. Uh..."

"Rachel. We don't use last names in this family. I'm just putting dinner out so I expect to see you both as soon as you finish up there."

"Yes, ma'am," Larry said, snapping a salute. The main viewer went blank. "Hope you don't mind family get-togethers," he added as he unbuckled his safety restraints. "I just need to go through the post-landing checklist with the controller, but you can go out and stretch your legs if you want."

"Sure. How long will it take?"

"Just five minutes or so if nothing needs adjusting. Aarden's gravity is around eight percent higher than Earth standard, so don't be surprised if you feel a bit heavy."

Georgia wasn't sure if she really felt the weight differ-ence on her arms going down the ladder or if it was psychosomatic. She found that the ramp was already descending when she got to the bottom, meaning that Larry must have instructed the controller to do it for her. She barely had a chance to breathe in a lungful of fresh air before a woman who appeared to be in her early sixties approached.

"Georgia?"

"Rachel?"

"I was hoping you'd come out first. Once Larry and his father start talking Guild politics we won't be able to get a word in edgewise. So how long have the two of you been together?"

"You mean me and Larry?" Georgia hesitated for a moment because she hated to disappoint Larry's mother. "I'm a paying passenger. I work for the Galactic Free Press and I needed a way to follow the Colony One ship around."

"Sally's group? Whatever for?"

"I'm trying to get into investigative journalism and I thought Colony One was a scam."

Rachel burst out laughing. "Oh, that's funny. I'll have to tell Sally. I'm planning on taking the elevator up tomorrow to meet her."

"You know the head of Colony One?"

"I think she prefers Captain Sally now, but when you're rich, you can get away with those minor affectations."

"Rich? Do you mean Colony One is collecting money after all?"

"The opposite, my dear. You're too young to remember her, but she used to be known as Sally Nugget."

"The woman who discovered the solid gold asteroid? I heard about that when I was a child."

"It wasn't really an asteroid, mind you, just a big chunk of gold that had probably been part of some ship's cargo a hundred million years ago, but nobody ever presented a counter-claim. It wasn't worth anywhere near the trillion creds the Grenouthian News made it out to be either, but she was able to retire from trading before she really got started. I knew her before I married Phil and she found her pot of gold. Sally spent a few decades cruising around the tunnel network as a tourist after that, and she came back with this idea that humanity needed a colony ship of its own."

"So the whole thing is philanthropy?"

"That's a good word for it," Rachel agreed. "Sally couldn't have children because of a radiation accident when she was young, and she wanted to do something for future generations with her money."

"Why didn't Larry say anything to me about her?" Georgia asked.

"I'm sure he didn't know. I hadn't heard from Sally for years myself, and I only found out she was behind Colony One when she contacted me to say she would be coming here. She knew that I would never miss a Rendezvous."

"I'm going up myself for the tour of Flower that Colony One is sponsoring. I'm hoping to manage at least one story that isn't about food out of this trip. Are you taking the elevator?"

"Of course. If you promise not to ask any of those hard-nosed reporter questions, I'll introduce you to her."

"I'd love that."

"And I'd love to hear more about you and Grumpy," Rachel insinuated.

"Grumpy? Do you mean your son? He's been very nice to me."

"Maybe he's finally getting over it. Did he tell you about his ex?"

"Only to say he didn't want to talk about it."

"It was our fault, really, by which I mean my husband's fault. He and Thistle's father are old friends—they operated a two-man trader together when they started out. Larry and Thistle grew up hearing from their fathers how perfect they were for each other, and they were always inseparable when we met up. They even got married at a Rendezvous."

"What happened?"

"Thistle was always a bit, well, let's just say she liked to get her way. When she was ten, it was sort of cute. By the time she turned twenty, I had my misgivings, but Larry didn't seem to mind. It only took her a year of marriage to decide she had made a mistake. Larry was heartbroken as well as nose-broken since he never saw it coming, and I don't think he's looked at another woman since she left."

"Oh. Well, I think he's very nice."

Rachel groaned. "Nice?"

"More than nice," Georgia amended herself, "but we have a working relationship and I don't want to mess that up. Besides, he's never given me the slightest sign."

"If you're hoping my son will share his feelings first you're both in for a long wait. Forgive me for presuming, but do you mind if I give you a piece of advice?"

"Please do."

"Get him drunk," Rachel said, and then smiled over Georgia's shoulder. "There you are, Phil. Come and meet Larry's passenger."

After a quick introduction, Larry's father asked the reporter, "Did you come for Rendezvous? It's going to be a wild one this year."

"I was traveling with Larry chasing a story that didn't pan out and I thought I'd write a few articles about trader food culture while I'm here. I'm a freelancer for the Galactic Free Press."

"Do you cover the Conference of Sovereign Human Communities? The council election next week will determine whether the Traders Guild will become a member."

"Larry told me all about it while we were exercising in Zero-G. There's a full-time reporter on Union Station who covers CoSHC, but I'm afraid I haven't paid very close attention. I'm not sure I understand why so many traders are reluctant to join."

"Old minds, old ways," Rachel put in.

"We actually looked into it a few years ago, but some of the CoSHC members at that time didn't believe that the Traders Guild rises to the level of a community," Phil explained. "I've been on the council for over twenty years and I'll admit that we're a pretty independent bunch, but it doesn't take the Prophet Nabay to see which way the human diaspora is heading. I'm stepping down because I'm too old a dog to learn a new trick, but Larry is running on the pro-CoSHC platform for my seat, and I think most of my old supporters will line up behind him."

"Is it a full-time job, being on the council?" Georgia asked.

Rachel and her husband exchanged a look and burst out laughing.

"Did I miss a good joke?" Larry asked as he joined the group.

"I was just curious whether you'd have to stop trading if you win your father's council seat."

"It's nothing like that. The council only meets once a year at Rendezvous, though if we do join the Conference of Sovereign Human Communities, I suppose somebody will have to act as our representative. But CoSHC only has the one convention a year, and most of the business is done over the Stryxnet."

"In all the time Phil has been on the council, I doubt he ever put in more than a couple days a year while we weren't at Rendezvous," Rachel said.

"So how do the traders know who to vote for?" Georgia asked.

"It's basically a popularity contest," Larry told her. "Most of the council members have either been traders for decades or they grew up in it, like me."

"But still, how many people could actually know you? There must be hundreds of thousands of independent traders."

"A couple of million, at least, but you have to be at Rendezvous to vote. I have twelve days to convince voters, and the election is on the last night. It pretty much comes down to the speeches."

"Haven't you noticed what a beautiful speaking voice my son has?" Rachel teased.

"The Traders Guild is less one big community than a collection of smaller groups," Phil said. "Those of us who trade the same routes or make our home port different places tend to get to know each other. My friends and I will be talking up Larry, and his friends will do the same. By the way, I stopped at Chintoo orbital and got you ten thousand printed markers at wholesale. You owe me four hundred creds."

"Twenty-five markers to the cred is dirt cheap," Larry said. "Are they any good?"

"The artificial Sharf who handled the printing guaranteed they're the same product he makes for Mark-Up, but without the branding, of course. Give it a shot." Phil drew from his pocket two cylinders about as wide around as Georgia's pinky and twice as long and handed them over.

"Vote for Larry, Phil's son," Georgia read the printed message on the side of the marker. "That's pretty straightforward."

Larry removed the cap and sniffed the soft tip of the marker. "Yup. Smells just as bad as a Mark-Up." He drew a line on the back of his hand, recapped the marker, and then flipped it over. "Now comes the real test," he said, and ran the flat end of the marker over the line he had just drawn. It disappeared completely.

"What do traders use these for?" the reporter asked.

"Didn't you notice all of the printing on containers and crates in my cargo?"

"I just didn't make the connection because I never saw you writing on anything. Can it erase lines after they dry?"

"Everything would be covered with cross-outs by now if they didn't. Thanks, Dad. Between your friends and my friends, we should get most of them handed out in time for the election."

"But take a look at these," Phil said, pulling a rectangular package out of his back pocket.

"Playing cards?" Larry examined the smiling woman's face on the box and then extracted the deck of cards. "Beth Anderson? I've never heard of her. Is she on every—they're all different!"

"Actually, each candidate repeats through all four suits for the same value of card, and the face on the box gets the jokers as well. So the opposition has a candidate standing for all thirteen council seats and they're running as a package deal."

"These are pretty nice cards, other than the faces," his son said, executing a one-handed cut and tossing an arc. "Somebody spent some money."

"They're giving these away all around Rendezvous," Rachel informed her son. "I picked up that deck at the Vergallian market this morning when I went to buy fresh vegetables. All of the vendors were giving them away. I asked one girl who was running her family's farm stand, and she said that a Human came around last week and offered all of the vendors twenty creds a day to give them out."

"Somebody has deep pockets," Larry observed as he worked his way slowly through the deck, studying the images. "You know, I don't recognize a single one of these traders."

"Neither did we," Phil said. "And they all use two names, which pretty much tells you that they're first-generation."

"Do traders really elect council members based on pens and playing cards?" Georgia couldn't help asking.

"We never took it that seriously because the council doesn't have any power, other than managing Rendezvous. But the Conference of Sovereign Human Communities addressed the invitation to us, so all of a sudden, the council is a battleground."

A young woman on a bicycle turned into the campsite and braked to a halt right next to the pair of couples. "Hi," she said with a bright smile. "Do you have a minute to talk?"

"Maureen?" Larry asked, working his way back a few cards and then pulling one out and holding it up to compare the image with the original.

"That's me," Maureen said. "As you know, I'm running for the council, and I just wanted to introduce myself and ask for your vote."

"Have you been a trader long?" Rachel inquired. "We come to Rendezvous every year, and I have a good memory for faces, but I don't recall meeting you."

"It's my first Rendezvous, but I've had my ship for six years now. I never thought I'd be running for the council, but I became a trader for the independent lifestyle, and I'm totally against joining the royalty thing."

"Conference of Sovereign Human Communities," Georgia told her. "It's an elective body that—"

"You know what I mean," Maureen interrupted. "They claim to be sovereign, but most of their communities are on so-called open worlds that belong to alien empires. Sure, there are over thirty million humans here on Aarden, but the world is ruled by a Vergallian queen." She lowered her voice and made a show of checking the surroundings before continuing. "I heard that the last council got paid to move Rendezvous here after the Stryx opened the tunnel."

"Have a marker," Phil said, handing one to the young woman. "I'm the father, by the way."

"You're running for the council?" Maureen asked Larry, her face flushing red. "Why didn't you say so?"

"You were doing such a good job telling us the way it is that I didn't want to interrupt," Larry said. "Word of advice. If you want to be taken seriously, talk more about the trading you've done and leave the conspiracy theories to Earthers."

Maureen stood on the pedals to get the bike moving, and Rachel made a rude gesture at her back. "Coming onto my campsite and insulting my husband. I should have slashed her tires."

"She didn't wait around long enough," Georgia said. "Do you think that all of the candidates on the playing cards are out on bicycles doing the same thing?"

Phil frowned. "I don't remember ever seeing election swag that promoted more than one person. Most years it's a struggle just to get enough candidates to stand. Rachel?"

"It's something new, all right, but we can worry about it after we eat," she said, ushering the group in the direction of the fold-out picnic table. "Tell us what you think of the trading life, Georgia. Is the time you spent with my son your first experience in a small ship?"

"Yes, and other than the first bout of Zero-G sickness, I loved it. I even got to save the ship from a saboteur," she added proudly.

"What happened?" Rachel demanded of her son. "You're not the first candidate to have a problem."

"Somebody slipped a chewer on the ship and it went after the secondary cooling hoses," Larry said. "I didn't want to pull up all the deck plates, and Georgia was able to work her way through and crush it. What do you mean we weren't the first?"

"Kari's ship was holed when she was approaching Aarden," Phil told him grimly.

"Kari the gardener? The woman who's sat on the council longer than anybody?"

"Hit by a steel ball bigger than the meteor protection field or the self-sealing hull could handle. Luckily, Kari was on her cargo deck when it happened, and she had the hatch closed because she's religious about sealed compartments. Kari laughed it off as a trillion-to-one-shot bit of space junk, but it's pretty obvious that somebody potted her with a rail gun. And Arlene said she would be here early to discuss strategy but she's a day overdue."

"Everybody likes Arlene," Larry protested.

"Is she running for reelection to the council too?" Georgia asked.

"She planned to, but the deadline for registration is in two days, and candidates have to be here in person," Phil said. "Rachel, you give the kids dinner. I'm going to round up the other council members who are here and see if we can work out exactly what is going on."

Fourteen

"Thank you again for all of the help," Ellen said to Marshall. "I wouldn't have even known about this long-term lot for traders if you hadn't told me. And the meeting facility was a life-saver when the representatives of all the different journalist groups from around the world flew in to finalize our syndication deal this morning. I was going to rent a meeting room at a hotel, but this was much nicer."

"If you missed the plaque, the meeting hall was a gift from Drazen Foods," Marshall told her. "It's a tradition of theirs to build facilities for independent traders at the ground stations of space elevators on all of their own worlds. When they saw that Earth didn't have one, they offered to take care of it."

"The ironic thing is that I'm on an expense account for the first time in my life, yet I'm being more careful with my programmable cred than when I'm footing the bills myself."

"If you come back to Earth frequently enough it's worth paying for the annual parking pass. The break-even is around thirty days, and if you're going to be returning here once a month to meet with the journalists in your new syndicate, you'll save some creds."

"The Galactic Free Press thanks you," Ellen said. The opening chords of Beethoven's Fifth played from her back pocket and she pulled out her cell phone. "Hello?" Her expression changed to one of disgust and she tapped the disconnect.

"Telemarketing call?" Marshall asked sympathetically. "I pay extra for a service that blocks them if you want me to give you the details. Earth must be the only planet in the galaxy that allows communications spam, but they cling to the old cell phone network as a matter of pride."

"Prank call," Ellen told him. "Some clown saying he's the President of EarthCent." The phone rang again, and this time the freelancer said, "Jerk," before hanging up.

"How do you know it's not actually the president?" Marshall asked.

"Why would the president call me? Besides, nobody that high up would place a call themselves. They'd have a secretary do it."

Beethoven's Fifth began to play again, and Marshall said, "Let me have a look."

Ellen handed the phone over, and before he answered, the trader tapped an icon she'd never noticed, and then held the device a couple of feet in front of his face as the video function went live.

"Hello? Yes, it is her phone. Yes, Mr. President. Yes, she's right here." He handed the phone back to Ellen, who blushed like a schoolgirl.

"I'm so sorry about calling you a jerk," she began. "I thought you were a prankster."

"Happens all the time," the EarthCent president assured her. "I just got off a tunneling network conference call about a promotion we're running in conjunction with the Galactic Free Press at Rendezvous this year. Your managing editor, Walter Dunkirk, participated as well. Our head of public relations, Hildy Greuen, decided at the last minute that she'd like to attend Rendezvous in person,

163

but there isn't a direct passenger service from Earth to Aarden. Walter mentioned that you were just wrapping up some business here and would probably be leaving for Rendezvous later today."

"EarthCent's head of public relations wants to hitch a ride on my ship?"

"We'll pay," the president offered hopefully.

"I'm not worried about that, it's just—it's a two-man trader. The trip to Aarden will take almost forty-eight hours in the tunnels, all of that in Zero-G, and—"

"Hildy is an experienced traveler. Whenever we go somewhere, I'm the one who gets sick."

"I was just packing up to leave," Ellen said irresolutely. "I already reserved a slot with—"

"She's at the base of the elevator now so she could take the monorail to your location and be there in less than twenty minutes. You'll be saving her a full day on the elevator, and at least three days travel."

"Okay. Give her my number so we can do the location thing when she gets here."

"EarthCent owes you a debt of gratitude," the president said. "If you ever get caught up in customs, give me a call."

"Earth doesn't have customs."

"We're working on it."

Ellen turned to Marshall after the call disconnected and found the older trader smiling broadly. "What?"

"You hung up on the President of EarthCent twice," he told her. "I've been wondering where I was going to come up with a new story to tell at the Rendezvous competition. I'll have to embellish a little, but it's got great potential."

"I'm not sure it's something I want to be known for."

"Could you give me a hand with the shade tent? I can take it down myself, but it's faster with two."

"Of course," Ellen said, and in ten minutes, the standard canopy deployed by human traders who made frequent visits to planetary surfaces was folded up and stored away in the hold.

"It was a pleasure meeting you, Ellen, and I hope to see you at Rendezvous," the older trader said. "I have an open slot from the tunnel controller so I may as well get going."

"An open slot? How come I had to reserve a time?"

"You didn't, but if you contact the controller ahead and ask for a reservation, the AI will make one for you. They aim to be accommodating. If you're all packed up, you have just enough time to walk to the monorail station to meet your guest. I noticed that the battery on your phone is running down. I don't know if it will last long enough for her to find you if it has to broadcast the location beacon."

"Thanks again for everything," Ellen said, and after commanding her ship controller to secure the vessel, she started for the monorail station. Behind her, Marshall's ship silently ascended into the sky, gathering speed as it went. Her phone rang just as she reached the switch-back ramp that rose to the elevated station.

"Hello?"

"Is this Ellen?"

"You must be Hildy. I walked over to the station to meet you."

"How very kind. I just arrived and I'm heading for the exit ramp."

"Can I come up and help you with your bags?"

"I travel light. Just look for the EarthCent hat."

Less than a minute later, Ellen saw a woman in her mid-fifties with an EarthCent baseball cap coming down the ramp with a single bag. The luggage wasn't even floating—just a hard-sided case with two wheels.

"Thank you for wearing your Galactic Free Press ID," Hildy said by way of greeting. "It's probably the only one on the planet, which makes it easy to pick you out in a crowd."

"The paper traditionally sources all of its Earth news from the teacher-bot newspapers and syndicated journalists, which is why they sent me here in the first place."

"Stephen told me he heard something about your mission from Chastity," the head of EarthCent's public relations said, falling in alongside the reporter, who took a moment to remember that the president's full name was Stephen Beyer. "And thank you for taking me on such short notice. I checked with the Vergallian travel agency that we normally use and commercial service to Aarden required a minimum of two connections."

"I've never flown commercial. My first experience in space came after I signed on as an apprentice with a trader who visited the world where I grew up."

"I hope it was a good experience," Hildy said, glancing over at the reporter. "I've heard some unfortunate stories, though I don't recall if they were from the news or an EarthCent Intelligence briefing."

"I was lucky," Ellen said. "I originally signed on with a woman whose husband had been her partner, but he decided he'd had enough of living in Zero-G and wanted to settle on a planet. They had already paid off the mortgage, so she took an equity loan to buy out his share, and was almost finished paying it down when I came along. I didn't receive any wages, but she gave me a percentage of the new stock to trade on my own account, which was the best education a trader can get. Then she got remarried and I did the last year of my apprenticeship with a man I met. We still keep in touch, and I hope to see her at Rendezvous."

Hildy took advantage of the opportunity to ask an unending stream of questions about the trading life, stopping only when they reached the ship and strapped in for departure. Ellen requested the minimum G-force lift-off from the controller, not wanting to take any unnecessary chances with her passenger's health. It was a costly move, in terms of her fuel pack, but probably no worse than if she had been stuck carrying the ore shipment she had convinced John to take for her.

By the time they reached the tunnel entrance, Hildy had shifted to questions about the news syndicate Ellen had just helped establish.

"So your paper's primary interest is expanding investigative journalism on Earth?" Hildy asked, and then added hastily, "Please stop me if you aren't comfortable answering."

"Not at all," the reporter said. "I can't believe I'm speaking with somebody so high up in EarthCent that she calls the president by his first name. It makes me feel like I have access or something."

"You do have access unless you lose our phone numbers, and then you can just contact the president's office. There are only a half-dozen of us working full-time on Earth. We rely on the tunnel-network ambassadors and their staffs to handle most of the diplomatic legwork, and EarthCent Intelligence is headquartered on Union Station."

"I just spent a month on your planet meeting journalists all over the globe and I still don't get how the government works. It seems to be a crazy patchwork of old nations and new city-states."

"That's a fair description," Hildy said. "I don't know if you're interested in history, but the bottom line is that when the Stryx opened Earth, they basically broke the historical power structure. The Stryx didn't attempt to dictate new laws to the existing leadership, but they made clear that interfering with emigration wouldn't be tolerated. When alien transports from different species began landing all over the world and recruiting contract labor, people realized they could vote with their feet, and they did."

"Well, Earth wasn't as bad as I expected, other than those irritating phone things. And now that I think about it, I didn't have a single contact with government at any level."

"That's pretty much how it works unless you're a resident," Hildy explained. "Then they start hitting you with fees for services, though technology has greatly reduced the number of government employees at all levels. Where Stephen and I live, we pay a monthly fee for public safety and education, but in less populated areas, it's common for children to study with teacher bots and only spend time in classrooms if there's parental involvement."

"I've heard that most of the governments went broke in the years after the Stryx opened Earth because their populations fell but the pensioners stayed."

"Yes, the first few decades were tough for people who remained behind. Remittances from family members working on alien contracts helped, and a combination of inflation and defaults eventually cleared away the debt burden. Some people think that conditions are only improving now because of all the alien businesses operating on Earth, but things have actually been on an upward path for decades. It's just a shame that a new concentration of wealth and power is leading to corruption."

"That was the conclusion of all the journalists I met with," Ellen agreed, stifling a yawn.

"I take it politics isn't your thing."

"What? Oh, I'm sorry, it's the tunnel," Ellen said. "For some reason, it always puts me to sleep. The boyfriend I finished my apprenticeship with had the opposite problem. As soon as we landed on a planet or docked with a spinning structure that gave him weight, he was falling asleep."

"You left him to buy your own ship?"

"I was freelancing for the Galactic Free Press by then, and when I left to chase a story, we just sort of drifted apart," Ellen said. "I think I'm going to pass out for a few hours. Do you know how to use a Zero-G bathroom?"

"I've traveled on Sharf traders before. I'll just hop on the exercise bike for a while if it won't bother you."

"Not at all. Feel free to eat anything you find."

By the time Ellen woke up, Hildy was passed out in her chair. The two women turned out to have completely opposite biorhythms, and they were only awake at the same time for around six hours of the trip, though part of this was due to the older woman's ability to sleep more than ten hours at a stretch. Coincidently, they were both up when the ship emerged from the tunnel and they were hailed by Aarden traffic control. After a brief negotiation, Ellen received landing coordinates for an open parking spot at Rendezvous.

"It feels like we've barely been traveling for a day," Hildy commented. "You're excellent company."

"Do you mean when I'm awake or when I'm sleeping."

"Both. You don't snore, in case nobody has ever told you."

"Thanks. Now that we're almost there, are you going to tell me about the big promotion EarthCent is co-sponsoring with my paper?"

"It's hardly a secret. It's just that public relations is my job, and once I get started talking about Earth, you can't turn me off. It basically comes down to trying to piggyback on the success the Grenouthians have had with their documentary tours for aliens. Those are focused on Earth history, of course, with visits to old battlefields, technology museums, and reenactment preserves."

"I heard of those, but I didn't get a chance to visit one."

"You may know that we licensed the Grenouthians to build documentary theme parks with human reenactors at three locations of their choice, one of which turned out to be an orbital studio complex. But the Grenouthians noticed that many cities around the world have abandoned sections which could be restored to earlier periods for less than building replicas, and they've been pouring money into doing just that. The bunnies have hired tens of thousands of locals to undergo training to reenact life in the seventeenth, eighteenth, and nineteenth centuries, which were all rich fodder for documentaries."

"And you want EarthCent to do the same?"

"Not at all," Hildy said with a laugh. "Besides, the Grenouthians weren't born yesterday, and they insisted on a monopoly before they started investing in the restorations. What I meant is that we want to promote Earth for destination vacations, but for humans rather than aliens. We're working on wedding venues, dude ranches, a Scottish Highlands paradise, religious pilgrimages—"

"A Scottish Highlands paradise?" Ellen interrupted.

"Time travel romance for the ladies, distilleries and caber tossing for the men. The point is, Earth has a lot to offer human tourists. Our deal actually touches on the news syndication work you're doing. Whenever a positive story about Earth runs in the Galactic Free Press, we'll pay to show our advertising alongside. I'm still fine-tuning the ad copy with focus groups, but some variation on, 'Come home for the vacation of your life,' will probably be the winner."

"That's catchy. But I thought that EarthCent was chronically broke and had no ability to raise revenue. Are the Stryx subsidizing the whole thing?"

"You haven't heard?" Hildy asked. "Our embassy on Union Station won the auction for the rights to the All Species Cookbook—your publisher and her sister put up the money. It's turned into an instant bestseller, and for the first time, we have a solid income stream that we can use for whatever we want without seeking Stryx approval. Ambassador McAllister has been licensing subsidiary rights for even more income, like the new Grenouthian cooking show, and a line of prepackaged ingredients to make the recipes. It's the first time I've ever had a real budget to do anything and I intend to take full advantage."

"But why is creating new business opportunities on Earth a priority?" Ellen asked. "After all, the only authority EarthCent has on the planet is granting extraterritorial status to alien business operations."

"For starters, we feel that it's important to keep expatriates connected to Earth in some way, just so they don't go so native that they forget that they're human. And even though over sixty percent of humanity now lives on other worlds, there are still more than four billion people on Earth, and four billion people without enough to do with

171

their time can cause a lot of trouble. I don't know if you read the EarthCent Intelligence report that was released in your paper, but most human criminality on the tunnel network can be traced directly to Earth."

"I did read that, but I didn't see much sign of it while I was there. Hey, I've got an extra hammock if you want to sleep on my ship once we're down. I'm going to grab the space elevator back up to Flower."

"Are you landing on Aarden just because of me?" Hildy asked. "If you want to stop on Flower for a few hours, I always like seeing how they're doing. I appreciate your hammock offer, but I've already agreed to stay with Fanny, if you know her."

"Everybody knows Fanny," Ellen said. "I'm landing because I reserved a spot at Rendezvous, and if I don't take it, you never know what will happen. Besides, I have a story to finish writing, and a long, boring elevator trip is the ideal place. I'll hitch a ride back down with somebody in a couple of days."

Fifteen

"Sally!" Rachel cried, and holding her arms up as if she was being robbed, rushed toward her old friend. The two women embraced, and then took a good long look at each other.

"I wish I could say you haven't changed a bit in thirty-five years," Sally said. "You look happy, though."

"I've had a good life and I'm not anywhere near ready to quit yet," Rachel replied. "You certainly haven't let any moss grow on you. How do you stay so thin?"

"Vergallian vegan," the president of Colony One said with a rueful smile. "It's actually very good if you travel in Vergallian space, but everywhere else—ugh."

"This is Georgia," Rachel introduced the reporter, who after discussing it with her host, had decided to wear her press ID in the open as usual. "She's with the Galactic Free Press, as you can see, and she came along for the tour."

"You look familiar," Sally said. "Did you attend one of our seminars?"

"On Poalim," Georgia said. "I had a misconception about your organization, but now I'm a big fan."

"Thought I was a scam artist, didn't you? I get that a lot, even from people who know I'm funding Colony One out of my own pocket. They think I want to set myself up as queen of a new world."

"But from everything I learned about the time involved to acquire a colony ship, you'll be, uh…"

"We'll all be dead by then," Sally said. "No need to beat around the bush about it. So, are you both looking forward to the tour? We can start anytime."

"I don't understand," Rachel said, looking around the docking bay where the shuttle from the elevator hub had deposited them. "Are we it?"

"Tours are starting continuously and around the clock. The colony ship's guiding AI, Flower, has deployed bots to lead the tours herself. There's a line of them waiting by the lift tube."

"That sounds like fun. We'll take the tour and then lunch is on me. I insist," Rachel said.

"You'll have to argue with Flower about picking up the check," Sally said as she led the way to the lift tube. "She's going all out with the welcome mat. I've already lost two of my staff."

"Lost? As in, you can't find them because they wandered off?"

"Lost as in Flower convinced them to immigrate, to remain on board. She's around four and a half million people under capacity, and running a ninety percent vacancy rate is bad for her bottom line. I cheated a little and took a quick tour last night. Can you guess where Flower brought me?"

"To the bridge," Georgia said immediately. "She must know who you are and she wanted to wow you."

"Flower brought me to an independent living cooperative for humans sixty-five and older. And I have to admit I was impressed, but I'm not quite ready to hang up my spurs yet."

"Three for the tour?" a floating four-armed robot inquired when the women reached the lift tube bank.

"That's right," Rachel said. "Are you artificial intelligence?"

"It's just a maintenance bot, but Flower controls them all directly," the founder of Colony One explained.

"Thank you, Sally," Flower said through the bot's speaker. "I know that you're Georgia Hunt because I read your press ID, but who might your companion be?"

"Rachel. Pleased to meet you."

"Are there any particular attractions you came to see or should I give you my standard tour?" Flower asked as the bot ushered the three women into the lift tube capsule.

"I saw in a Colony One brochure that the outer deck of Dollnick colony ships is always a reservoir," Georgia said. "I'd like to see how that works."

"Splendid," Flower said. "We'll start at the hull and work our way in, though it will take a few minutes to get there. What else did you learn from the Colony One brochure?"

"Well, I saw that Frunge colony ships are—"

"Deathtraps," the Dollnick AI interrupted. "I suppose with your short lifespans you might gamble on the cumulative effects of sub-par radiation screening, but then again, your DNA isn't as robust as that of the advanced species who've been traveling the stars for thousands of generations."

"Oh. Well, I thought that the Drazen colony ship—"

"More of a space-going hotel," Flower interrupted again. "Did you know that their current model has to tow in an orbital to do any serious terraforming work? I mean, what's the point of a colony ship if you get to your destination and you can't re-engineer the atmosphere."

175

Sally nudged Rachel and mouthed, 'All last night,' indicating that the conversation was a rerun for her.

"The Grenouthian design looked very comfortable," Georgia persisted. "Every deck was a park."

"The Grenouthians build a fine ship, the Verlocks as well for that matter, but let me ask you this," Flower continued, and lowered her voice in a conspiratorial fashion. "Would you buy a colony ship from a species that hasn't colonized a new world in over a hundred thousand years?"

"You mean they're just trophy ships?"

"Exactly. The Verlocks are too busy doing science and magic to be bothered with exploring anymore, and if the Grenouthians ever decide they want a new world, they'll run the numbers and find that it's cheaper to buy a custom job from us."

"Do any of the other species build a colony ship you would recommend?" Sally asked, winking at the other women.

"Well, the Cayl build an impressive vessel, but they keep them for themselves," Flower said grudgingly. "And here we are."

The lift tube doors slid open and the passengers exited onto a metal catwalk above a disconcerting lake. It took Georgia a moment to realize that there was something in the human psyche that rebelled against the idea of water sloping upwards to both the left and right, where it was held against the inner hull by centrifugal force.

"The lake extends all the way around your circumference?" Rachel asked.

"I'd be awfully out of balance if it didn't," Flower replied. "And it runs the full length of my axis as well. You can never have too much water aboard a colony ship, I always say."

"It's beautiful," Georgia said. "I wonder that it's not wall-to-wall tour groups."

"There are currently six hundred and thirteen visitors on the reservoir deck. I intentionally brought you all up through different lift tubes so you're either hidden from each other by the curvature of the deck or spaced out along the axis beyond your visual acuity."

"I heard that you have so much fresh fruit growing on board that you're giving it away," Rachel said.

"Samples, not bulk quantities," Flower corrected her. "If you've seen enough of the reservoir deck, I have something I want to show you."

"I thought you wanted us to tell you our interests," Sally said, and winked at the others a second time.

"One for you, one for me," the Dollnick AI responded. "It's only fair."

Flower's choice turned out to be a model residential cabin, which all three visitors had to admit was an extraordinary value for the price. Then it was their turn again, and Rachel requested to see the library, which supposedly hosted the largest collection of printed books in human languages anywhere in the galaxy. It must have been a popular spot on the tour because a young woman was waiting at the entrance and handing out pamphlets.

"Hi, I'm Julie," the greeter said. "Welcome to the library. We're running a special for people here on the colony ship tour. You can take a single book to keep free of charge, provided we have at least ten more copies in stock. And before you ask, books from the *For Humans* collection are excluded from this offer."

"How will we know if you have ten copies?" Sally asked.

"If you have a high-end implant, you can scan the code on the spine and the library stock will appear on your heads-up display," Julie replied. "We actually have hundreds of copies of the most popular books, but Dewey," she gestured at an odd-looking robot stationed behind the circulation desk, "will double-check when you leave. The books are all chipped, so if you, uh, put one in your purse and forget that it's there, the alarm will sound when you try to exit."

"Thank you," Sally said, accepting a brochure and leading the others into the library. "I actually have a book in mind, so can we agree to meet back at the circulation desk in fifteen minutes?"

Georgia and Rachel agreed, and after consulting the map in the brochure, the three women headed off in different directions. When they met up again, each had found a book to take home, and they compared their selections.

"Ten Days in a Mad-House," Rachel read off the title of the book Georgia had chosen when the freelancer handed it to the robot librarian for approval. "Doesn't sound very romantic."

"Somebody told me that it's a must for investigative journalists," she said. "I don't like reading from a tab on the exercise bike and Larry suggested I try paper."

"And what did you get?" Sally asked Rachel, peering at her old friend's selection. "Prince of the Highlands? He seems a bit underdressed for Scottish royalty, but it's nice to see that your taste hasn't changed."

"Don't show me yours, let me guess," Rachel said, dramatically placing a hand over her eyes. "Her Alien something-or-another, and the cover will have a picture of a blue-skinned male with six-pack abs and a woman kneeling at his feet."

"I'll have you know that she's standing next to him with their baby," Sally retorted.

Dewey confirmed that the women's selections were all overstocked, and as they exited the library Julie handed them a flier, this one promoting discounted medical services for tour participants. "The doctor is in," the girl called after them, just as a door on the corridor opened and a woman in her mid-thirties emerged.

"Ellen?" Georgia addressed her.

"I see from the ID that you're with the paper but I can't place you," the other reporter replied.

"Georgia Hunt, I used to be the food reporter on Union Station. We sat at the same table at the last awards dinner."

Ellen grimaced. "I don't really remember much of what happened that night. Did you get reassigned?"

"I've gone freelance," Georgia told her proudly. "Hey, can I buy you a meal and pick your brain? You were one of my inspirations to become an investigative journalist."

"Even after the awards ceremony? I'm afraid I was pretty blotto."

"You were brilliant, though. Rachel?" she called to the older woman, who had continued on a few steps and was laughing with Sally. "Do you mind if I drop out of the tour for a while and meet up with you later?"

"I'll ask Flower to ping you before I head back if you haven't caught up with us yet," Rachel said.

"It was nice to meet you," Sally added. "Be kind if you write an article about Colony One."

After consulting with Flower, the pair of reporters headed for the food court next to the bazaar and ended up at a lunch counter run by a towering four-armed Dollnick. It was only late morning and neither woman was particularly hungry, so they ended up ordering coffees and dessert.

"Did you come to Flower for the tour?" Georgia asked her companion.

"No. I was on board for part of her first circuit to write a series of articles. Flower and I are old friends."

"That was just before I was hired by the paper. It must have been exciting."

"It was different," Ellen admitted. "Are you here working on a story?"

"I just tagged along to meet Sally Nugget. My goal was to write a hard-hitting piece about financial fraud, but it turns out that Colony One is her philanthropy. She's very nice, and I'm making enough writing about food to cover the bills, so I've decided to start investigating all of the ship foreclosures going on instead. I never knew anything about the whole trader ecosystem before I started traveling with Larry and—"

"The Larry who's standing for the council?" Ellen interrupted.

"Yes. One of the women I was with is his mother."

"Then she must be Phil's wife. Are you writing about the election?"

"I messaged the freelance editor, Roland, but he replied that they already had somebody on it."

"Me," Ellen said. "I'm just finishing up a piece about the Advantage system that so many of the young traders are using and I'll be shifting to election coverage as soon as I return to Aarden." She examined the younger woman more closely. "It's your first time to Rendezvous?"

"Yes. This whole trip has been my first time away from Union Station since I left Earth."

"Rendezvous can get pretty crazy, with tens of thousands of traders showing up, and multiple events going on at the same time. I could use some help covering the election if you're willing to accept a 'written with' credit and the standard assist rate."

"Are you serious? I'd love that. I'm shocked that you'd trust me."

"Roland doesn't hire fools and I've read some of your restaurant reviews. Reporting on speeches is easier." Ellen took a forkful of pie, and Georgia noticed that the older reporter had a tremor in her hand.

"Are you alright?" Georgia asked, and then her memory flashed to the sign above the door Ellen had emerged from on the corridor that ended in the library. "You just came from the med bay."

"Yes. The doctor is a Farling, we met when I was here reporting Flower's first circuit. He offered to treat me then but I turned him down because I didn't think it was a big deal. I came back today to see if his offer was still good."

"Is that why you look a bit depressed? Did he refuse you?"

"No. He took samples from me and he needs to reprogram some nanobots to do the fine work. It will take him a few hours in his spare time, so I'll have to come back." Ellen shook her head as if she had promised herself to move on from that decision for the time being. "Did you say you were starting to investigate ship foreclosures?"

"Larry told me that they've been increasing this past year and Rendezvous seems like the ideal place to ask around. He said it was never a problem when most traders were buying second-hand ships direct from the Sharf, who held the mortgages, but I guess investors on Earth bought the notes somehow and now it's a mess."

"You can say that again," Flower contributed via an overhead speaker. "There have been attempts to repossess Sharf two-man traders parked on my docking deck, but I send my bots to see the repo men off. You should talk to the owners who are still on board."

"Were the foreclosures legally executed?" Georgia asked.

"Perhaps according to Earth laws, but I don't operate under their jurisdiction. Besides, what kind of bank loans money to somebody who can't repay it? From my perspective, the whole operation is fishy, and I told the representatives from MORE that if I see them again on my ship, I'll slap them in the brig."

"They'll complain to EarthCent," Ellen said.

"Let them waste their time if they want," the Dollnick AI said dismissively. "And if you know any traders who require financial sanctuary, I've got plenty of low-cost parking space."

"Can you contact the traders on board whose ships have been foreclosed on and tell them that reporters from the Galactic Free Press would like to meet them?"

"Consider it done," Flower replied. "I'll even give them time off from work if you'd like to do it while you're here today."

"You gave them jobs?" Georgia asked.

"A few of them have laid out their blankets in the bazaar and are doing business there, but most of them had already disposed of their goods at a loss in a desperate attempt to raise cash for their payments. And from what I saw, their inventories overlapped so badly that they were basically all competing to sell the same merchandise."

"Advantage," Ellen said. "The gist of my article is that the real purpose of the Advantage platform is to create losses for independent traders. I couldn't tie it directly to the rash of foreclosures, but I know that some of the repossessed ships are being transferred to a package delivery service based on Earth, and some of the traders who lost their ships signed on as operators."

"Follow the money," Flower advised them. "If you can put the mortgage consolidators in the same room with the people behind Advantage and the owners of the new package delivery service, you've got a story. Just get it done before the election."

"But that's in just another week," Georgia protested.

"My sources inform me that the faction running to keep the Traders Guild out of the Conference of Sovereign Human Communities is likely to win the election," the colony ship's AI continued. "They're well-funded and have been preparing their campaign for months."

"You're spying on the Guild?" Ellen asked.

"I'm listening in on people who are spying on the Traders Guild," Flower explained. "It's one of the advantages of being me."

Sixteen

"Down, Semmi! I'm sorry," John apologized to a trader who the gryphon had just mugged for a chilidog the man had barely tasted. "Let me buy you another."

"She's yours?" the trader asked, and began laughing so hard that he spilled half of the draft beer he held in his other hand. "You don't owe me a thing, brother. I'll be using this as the basis for my tall tale tonight. A human adopting a Tyrellian gryphon? I've never heard of such a crazy thing."

"I'm just babysitting," John protested, but the other trader had already turned away to order another chilidog.

Semmi burped and favored her temporary guardian with a "Feed me more," look that would have terrified a lesser man.

"I thought we agreed that you'd behave yourself if I let you out of the ship," John scolded the gryphon. "Do you want to spend the next week in your crate?" At the word, "crate," Semmi let out a whimper and curled up on the ground, making John feel like he had kicked a kitten. "Come on, then. I need to register before the deadline."

As the pair made their way through the crowd, John had to admit to himself that walking with a winged alien lioness that stood higher than his waist had its advantages. When they reached the registration tent, there was a line snaking around the corner, but one after another, all of the people waiting pleaded with John to just go ahead. When he reached the registration table, Semmi yawned, gave him a wink, and curled up for a catnap.

"Yes?" the old man behind the table inquired.

"John. I'm registering as a candidate."

"How many years a trader?"

"Sixteen."

"Are you a member of a party?"

"Since when do we have parties?"

"Since this year, but if you didn't know that, you're running as an independent."

"Of course."

"Do you want anything after your name on the ballot?"

"EarthCent Intelligence," John said, and the conversations in the line behind him suddenly trailed off.

"Excuse me?"

"I have a side job as a handler for EarthCent Intelligence. I run agents. Lots of traders have side jobs."

"Oh, you're *that* John. I've heard of you. And you're sure you want to reveal it on the ballot? Are you recruiting?"

"Always, but that's not the reason for full disclosure. I'm running for the council because I want the Guild to join the Conference of Sovereign Human Communities. It's only fair people know up front that I'm with EarthCent Intelligence so there won't be any accusations of election interference. I'm running for me, not my employers."

"All right, I know better than to contradict a man with a gryphon." The registrar tapped something out on his tab, then held it up to capture an image of John's face. Then he handed over a piece of yellow ribbon and said, "Tie that around your arm and you're all set. If you want to write a bio to go with the picture, your face is your password for accessing the edit mode."

"Thanks. Did registration just open?" John asked, indicating the line behind him. "It looks to me like there are at least three times as many candidates as I remember having to vote for in the past."

"Everybody else is here to register for the first night of the Tall Tales contest. The speeches by council candidates are basically a warm-up act to make the storytellers look good."

"Thanks," John said, nudging Semmi with his foot as he turned to go. Ignoring the beer tents, he led the gryphon to the fair, where thousands of traders had spread their blankets. Some were there to make deals, but most of the older traders were only showing one or two items, usually of alien manufacture. Judges were circulating looking for the most interesting artifacts, questioning the owners about how they were acquired, and taking images.

Semmi proved to be worth her weight in gold as an attention magnet, and John found himself wishing that he had added "Gryphon" rather than "EarthCent Intelligence" to his ballot entry.` He had an excellent memory for faces and was able to greet dozens of traders by name, not counting those who he had paid for information over the years. By the time dinner rolled around, Semmi had mooched so much food that she wasn't hungry, and when John suggested she might want to get some exercise, the gryphon lumbered into the air and began flying laps around the Rendezvous grounds. Not having begged any food for himself, John got into line for the bar-b-que.

"Are you speaking after the cookout?" asked a man whose nose looked like it had been broken in a fight and never been set properly.

"If there's time," John replied. "The registrar hinted that the Tall Tales contest has priority. I take it from the ribbon that you're running?"

"I'm Phil's son, Larry," the other trader introduced himself and offered a handshake.

"John, EarthCent Intelligence. I've done business with your father a few times over the years, a good trader."

"Since you're not wearing a playing card with a picture of you pinned to your shirt, I'll assume you're one of the good guys."

"Are you saying that the candidates running against joining CoSHC are giving away whole decks of cards?"

"Yup. The opposition is prepared and they've spent some serious creds on swag."

"So how many of them are there? Fifty-two?"

"They're running exactly thirteen candidates, one per seat."

"While our side risks diluting the vote over too many candidates," John said with a frown. "Maybe I should withdraw my name. I didn't discuss my plans with anybody beforehand, because in past elections, everybody ran as independents."

"As it happens, we're lucky you signed up because one of the current council members who was planning to run again isn't going to make it here in time," Larry said, shuffling a few steps closer to the grill. "The anti-CoSHC candidates are all pretty young and nobody seems to know much about them. It would have been nice if their biographies were printed on the backs of the playing cards, but as my dad pointed out, that would have made them useless for poker."

"A pre-marked deck that everybody can read." John snorted. "Did you prepare a speech for tonight?"

"A journalist friend helped me write one. You?"

"I've got a whole spiel I do for the casual agents I recruit for EarthCent Intelligence, and most of it applies."

"Do your best for humanity? That sort of thing?" Larry asked.

"You've heard it?"

"EarthCent is nothing if not consistent. Two burgers," he told the woman working the grill. "All the fixings."

"Same for me," John said. "Is everything...?"

"Vergallian vegan," the grill cook replied. "It's the real stuff, not what you get on alien worlds."

"You know, we probably shouldn't eat together," Larry said after they paid for their food.

"You're right," John agreed. "It's an opportunity to sit with some strangers and maybe scare up a few votes. I guess I'll see you when the speeches start. Do we put our names in a hat?"

"Yes, they'll announce it to everybody around an hour from now. Good luck."

The enormous hand-stitched dining hall tent that doubled as the main venue for speeches had obviously been manufactured on a tech-ban world in the Vergallian Empire. There were so many poles holding up the dark green canopy that it felt a bit like entering an old-growth forest that had been filled with hundreds of rows of folding tables and many thousands of folding chairs. John intentionally picked a table with just one open seat to maximize his number of fellow diners, and someone soon remarked on his yellow candidate ribbon.

"They asked me to stand for a seat," the young woman across from him said. "I told them that I'm against the council on principle. I mean, I get that Guild dues help make Rendezvous possible and pay the rental for this tent

188

and such," she added, pointing overhead with her fork, "but for me, it's less about whether the Traders Guild joins the Conference of Sovereign Communities than about the price of ships."

"Did you say somebody tried recruiting you to run?" John asked.

"A representative for the finance company that holds the mortgage on my Sharf trader suggested it. I finished my apprenticeship eight months ago, and I had enough saved for a down payment on a second-hand trader, but it turned out the Sharf are running out of them. The price is up more than twenty percent in just the last year. I had to partner up to get the deal done."

"The Sharf are running out of used two-man traders?"

"That's what the dealer in Earth orbit said," a young man two spots to John's left contributed. "I guess that after seventy or eighty years of demand, we've soaked up all of their excess inventory."

"I actually looked at a new model, but it costs five times as much, and the Sharf say we don't live long enough to qualify for a mortgage," the young woman across from John continued. "When the MORE reps approached me at Echo Station and asked me to run for the council, I told them I was too busy keeping up with my mortgage payments to spend my week at Rendezvous running for election. I got the feeling they might have offered me some kind of deal if we hadn't been on my ship where the controller was recording everything, but after my experience with Advantage, I don't trust anything those people say."

"Advantage sucks," a different woman at the table commented. "It starts you off with some solid trade suggestions that are probably stolen from the Verlock's

Raider/Trader platform, but as soon as you're willing to commit serious creds, it puts you into losing situations." As the woman spoke, she held up a tab in one hand, swiping her way through the candidate selection until she matched John's image with his face. "So what are you going to do about it, Mr. EarthCent Intelligence?"

"Just so everybody understands, I'm running for the council because I want to see the Guild join CoSHC," John replied. "But I can tell you that one of the main functions of EarthCent Intelligence is maintaining a database of businesses and services for our subscribers, and we've committed significant resources to investigate reports of shady refi deals and the factors contributing to a recent rise in mortgage defaults. In recent decades, the percentage of new traders failing their first year in business was below three percent, but in the past twelve months it's spiked above sixteen percent. That's not the sort of thing that goes unnoticed."

"So why haven't you gotten to the bottom of it yet?"

"Traders make up less than a tenth of a percent of Earth expatriates and we have to focus our limited resources where they'll have the most impact," John said. "We're just getting a handle on the crooked labor contractors whose activities impact hundreds of millions of people, and our current focus is on sketchy operators in the space mining industry."

"Yeah, I pity the poor souls who go into asteroid pro-specting," an older man at the table interjected, and then he launched into a long story about a palladium find in the Hargreaves system that became more improbable by the minute.

"Is that your story for the contest?" a young man inter-rupted the raconteur, who had paused for breath after explaining how he sealed a hull breach with a can of baked beans in heavy tomato sauce.

"This really happened to me," the storyteller replied, but he failed to maintain a straight face. "Or maybe it happened to my brother, it's getting hard to remember with all the new details."

"Is that a synonym for embellishments?"

"Hey, if the contest was about telling the truth, a robot would win every year."

"Attention all candidates," a voice rang out from the speakers positioned high on every tent pole. "If you wish to take the stage tonight, it's time to come up to the event desk and put your name in a hat. And will the owner of the Tyrellian gryphon with a sweet tooth please report to the event desk as well. Bring your programmable cred."

"That's me," John said, getting up from his spot. "I hope when it comes time to vote, you'll remember my face."

"I'll remember the expression on it when the announcer said, 'Bring your programmable cred,'" the storyteller replied. "Your gryphon?"

"Long story," John said. "Don't worry, I won't be entering the Tall Tales contest."

A woman wearing a hat branded "Myka's Chocolate Chip Cookies" was waiting at the desk with Semmi, who had a plastic bucket on her head.

"Whoever stuck the bucket on my gryphon's head better start running now," John growled.

"She already tried that once, but she ran into my table and dumped six trays of cookies on the ground," the baker shot back. "Your gryphon put the bucket on all by herself."

"Oh, sorry about that. Are they salvageable?"

"The cookies? They were individually wrapped so they're fine."

"Then what do I owe you for? The bucket of— molasses?" he asked, reading the upside-down label.

"No, the bucket was almost empty. She got into that fix licking it out."

"Then why the programmable cred?"

"I was just trying to scare you off. If nobody claimed the gryphon, I would have kept her. She seems like a sweetheart."

"Then why didn't you take the bucket off her head?" John asked.

"It's stuck," Myka said. "I did poke some holes in it along the edge to make sure she can breathe, but I don't really know how her head is shaped. I've never really seen a gryphon in the flesh before."

John crouched down in front of the winged lioness, who was acting very nonchalant about the whole affair, though that might have been the aftereffect of knocking her head into a table. "You really can't get that thing off yourself?" he asked.

The bucket shook from side to side.

"I can try pulling it off, but it might hurt. Less risky than cutting, though."

The wings shrugged.

John sat on the ground and braced his feet against the gryphon's shoulders, then grabbing the lip of the bucket on each side, began to pull. The bulge in the plastic wall of the bucket began to move slowly back from the bottom, and then the whole thing came free at once, propelling John into a backward somersault that he somehow ended on his feet.

Everybody at the front of the tent burst into applause, and Semmi began to preen her ruffled feathers back into place.

"You've got my vote," a trader shouted, though John didn't know if the pledge of support was for him or the gryphon.

Another one of the diners matched John's face to the candidate list on his tab and called out, "Does everybody who signs up with EarthCent Intelligence get a killer pet?"

The gryphon snapped her beak at this remark, and John hastened to calm her. "He wasn't talking about you, Semmi."

Larry tapped John's shoulder to get his attention. "Putting your name in the hat? It looks like all thirteen anti-CoSHC candidates are already signed up, plus most of our side."

"Where's the hat?"

"Here," Larry said, passing over a tab with a picture of a hat on the screen. "Just take a selfie and it will figure out the rest."

John held the tab in front of his face, angling it self-consciously for the least distorted image, and then he staggered as a heavy weight pushed on both shoulders and a beaked face with a lolling tongue appeared next to his own. He tapped the blinking button anyway, handed back the tab, and then pried the gryphon's paws off his shoulders.

"Down, Semmi," he said, to reinforce the message.

"Are you taking her on stage with you for the speech?" Larry asked.

"Do you think it would be a good idea?"

"People will certainly remember you," the other trader said, returning the tab to the woman running the event desk. "If I was you, I'd swap that picture for the one they took at the registration desk."

"Can we do that?"

193

"I already did it for mine. You just go to the page on your own tab, hit the 'edit' option, and scan your face for the password."

"I'll do that tonight. When do we find out who speaks when?"

"Right now," the woman at the desk said. She swiped an option on the tab and the two dozen or so pictures all swirled together before rearranging themselves in a grid in ranked order. Then the event coordinator tapped a pin on the collar of her blouse and began to speak in the professional-announcer voice they had heard over the public address system a few minutes prior.

"There are twenty-three candidates registered to speak tonight, and as this event is scheduled for two hours, each will be given five minutes maximum." Then she began reading off the order, and John found himself stuck in the last slot, immediately following Larry.

"What kind of random drawing was that?" Larry asked the women. "We were the last two candidates to sign up, and the first thirteen are all from the anti-CoSHC party."

"The early Dolly gets the Sheezle bug," she replied philosophically. "You can always complain to the outgoing council."

The speeches didn't start for another half hour, by which time at least two-thirds of the crowd had wandered off to the fair. The thirteen candidates from the anti-CoSHC party all proved to be attractive younger traders, and they offered up impressive, if somewhat similar speeches, every one of them starting with a joke and ending with a promise of independence and prosperity.

The next eight speakers were all current council members standing for reelection, and they spoke in favor of joining the Conference of Sovereign Human Communities.

194

By the time Larry's turn came, the tent had begun filling up again for the storytelling contest that would follow, so going on near the end proved to be a blessing in disguise. Larry spent a couple of minutes talking about growing up in a trading family and his years operating his own ship. He concluded with a well-reasoned argument for why the best way for traders to ensure their continued independence was to have representation in CoSHC, which was one day likely to become the off-Earth government for most of humanity. Then he left the stage and John took his place, the gryphon following at his heel.

"I'll be the last candidate before we move on to the Tall Tales contest that I know you're all really here for, so I'll try to be brief," John began.

Semmi yawned ostentatiously, then curled up and covered her head with a wing, drawing a roar of laughter from the crowd.

"Thank you, Semmi," he continued. "There's a story about a village on Earth, hundreds of years before the Stryx opening, where parents tried to choose who their children would marry. There was no greater shame in this community than when a child rejected that choice and ran off to escape parental control. When young people began disappearing from the village one after another, their families tried to keep it a secret so as not to be shunned by their neighbors. Nearly a year passed before a young woman made it home after escaping from the city where she'd been sold as a slave."

"The gryphon must have heard it before," a heckler called out.

"My point is, if the parents hadn't been so intent on keeping their shame to themselves, the villagers would have figured out much quicker that slavers were kidnapping and selling their children. Independent traders fall into the same trap, holding our cargoes, costs, and travel plans close to the vest, because in one sense, we're competing with each other. But in another sense, we're all one family, and without sharing information, we can't protect ourselves from coordinated attacks by forces that prey on independents."

"Are you trying to recruit informers for EarthCent Intelligence?" somebody shouted.

"What I'm getting at is that the Conference of Sovereign Human Communities is, above all else, an information-sharing organization. For years they wouldn't consider accepting the Traders Guild as a member, and some of us were angry about that, and maybe now that makes us want to reject their offer. But CoSHC is a player on the human stage in a way that the Guild alone can never be, and we'll be stronger with them than on our own." John paused a moment to gather his thoughts, and Semmi peered up at him from under her wing, as if to ask if he had finished.

"That's the first political speech I've ever made and I hope you enjoyed it more than the gryphon," he concluded.

Seventeen

"Welcome home," Larry greeted his paying passenger. "I was beginning to worry that you and my mom had decided to stay up there. I've heard that Flower can be very persuasive."

"It was a lot of fun," Georgia said, and passed Larry a box that was surprisingly heavy for its size. "I don't know where you want to keep this, but it's a soaked fruitcake, a gift from Flower. Supposedly they're best if aged for at least six months."

Larry opened the locker where he stored canned goods and wedged the cake into the top shelf. "Don't let me forget it's in there."

"I ran into a famous freelancer from the Galactic Free Press while we were on Flower, and she asked me to work with her on a story about traders refinancing their mortgages and losing their ships. Would it reflect badly on you if I tag along while you campaign and try to get interviews?"

"I'm fine with it, and I can't see anybody not voting for me because you're doing research. They can always refuse to answer."

"Great. I'll even kiss babies for you. Just let me grab a bite of breakfast first."

"Just hold that thought and come with me. Our first stop this morning is Fanny's Famous Pancake Breakfast.

It's an annual event at Rendezvous and all of the candidates are expected to show up. Fanny's like a hundred years old."

"Don't let her hear you say that," the freelancer advised. She topped off her large purse with felt-tipped markers printed 'Vote for Larry, Phil's son,' and then followed the candidate down the ladder from the bridge and out the cargo hatch. Larry ordered the controller to secure the ship and led them deeper into the campground. "How can you tell where we're going?" Georgia asked.

"Fanny and her family operate a converted Drazen supply ship she traded for around thirty years ago. It's the tallest ship in the trade fleet. See?" He pointed at a vessel that stood head and shoulders above the surrounding ships, most of which were of the two-man Sharf variety.

"It's huge," Georgia marveled. "I didn't know humans were allowed to operate ships that big."

"There aren't any rules about ownership, it's just a matter of what we can afford," Larry explained. "Fanny is old enough to be one of the original independent traders and she's smart enough to have made a lot of money. Rather than retiring, she put her creds into a ship with twenty decent-size cabins and plenty of room for cargo. Everybody you see serving pancakes today is a member of her family."

Somebody had rented a hundred folding picnic tables for the event, but even so, there were plenty of people left eating while they stood. That worked well for the candidates, who preferred to circulate and meet as many people as possible. Georgia took advantage to keep asking younger traders about refinancing until she came across a young man who was more than eager to share his story.

"I'm Daryl, and I'll talk on the record," he told her immediately. "Those bastards stole my ship on Braaken while I was at the local trade grounds. When I got back—"

"Hold on a second," Georgia begged him. "Do you mind if I record this on my tab?"

"Please do," Daryl said, and waited for her to get out her Galactic Free Press tab and set the mode. "As I was saying, I was trading on Braaken, and when I got back to the parking area, my ship was gone with all my stuff on board. At first I thought it had been jacked by choppers, but there was—"

"Choppers?" Georgia interrupted again.

"You know, thieves who steal ships to chop them up for parts. Anyway, a trader I know who was parked nearby came running out and gave me a sheaf of paperwork. Actual paper, can you believe that? She tried to stop the repo team from taking the ship, but they told her that I'd defaulted on the mortgage and they were engaged in a lawful repossession. I didn't even know that they had the override codes for the controller, but it turns out all of that stuff was included in the original Sharf mortgage data."

"So your mortgage was one of those bundled into a security—"

"About ten months ago I got conned in a deal for fuel packs," Daryl spoke over her. "The seller rigged them out with thin-film battery overlays in the power ports, so when I tested them, they read over eighty percent of the life left. I should have known something was wrong because the asking price was too low, but the guy had a sob story about needing cash to cover *his* mortgage, and I got greedy and blew all of my operating capital on them. A day after I realized I'd been had, the reps from MORE showed up and offer me a refi deal."

"I didn't quite understand what happened with the fuel packs," Georgia said. "Those thin-film batteries you talked about. Are they alien technology?"

"Verlock, I think. I found out later that most species use them in tabs, but a fuel pack holds like a trillion times more power than a thin-film battery—it's completely different technology. I only found out when I sold the first fuel pack to another trader and he didn't even make it off the ground. It's lucky for me that ship controllers test the reserve capacity when they power up or I might have been guilty of murder. As it is, the guy socked me in the jaw for being an idiot, and I deserved it."

"So just to recap, you spent all of your cash on fuel packs that turned out to be worthless, and then MORE reps happened to show up and offer you a lifeline."

"At the time I was like, 'Thank you, thank you,' but the payment schedule left no room for error, and when I tried the new trading platform—"

"Advantage?" Georgia interjected.

"Disadvantage is more like it. Within six months of the refi, I was selling at cost to try to raise cash for payments. Now I'm just another shipless bum at Rendezvous hoping somebody has room for a thirty-one-year-old apprentice so I can start over again."

"Did you report it to anybody? EarthCent Intelligence?"

"About the fuel packs? I put the word out on the trader network, but I'm sure the guy was using a fake name and probably a disguise. It's easy with Horten facial gel to pass as somebody else for a few days."

"I meant about the MORE reps showing up right after it happened."

Daryl's face turned pale. "You believe they set me up? The timing seemed suspicious when I thought about it later, but I figured I was just being paranoid. I wouldn't even be telling you this now if it wasn't for the guy with the cool gryphon at the Tall Tales competition last night. He's right about sharing information. If all of your readers laughing at me for being a sucker is what it takes to keep some other trader from losing his ship, I've got a thick enough skin for that."

"Thank you, Daryl. And I don't think anybody will laugh at you," Georgia said. "Oh, and take a marker," she added, producing one from her purse.

"As if I had something to write on, but beggars can't be choosers," the trader said. "Speaking of which, I'm going for another round of free pancakes."

"Good interview?" Larry asked her after the grounded trader got back in line.

"A couple more like that and we'll have this story wrapped up before Rendezvous is over," she said. "How are you making out?"

"Our opponents are giving away more than playing cards," Larry replied grimly. "One woman showed me a token that's good for twenty creds off her next mortgage payment if their side wins. Somebody has deep pockets."

"Isn't that illegal?"

"There was never really any competition for seats before, and some years, my dad and the old hands had to beg their friends to stand as candidates to round out the number. Why would the Guild need rules about buying votes when they couldn't give away the seats on the council?"

"I guess. What are they doing?" she asked, pointing at the ramp leading up to the hold of Fanny's ship. People were beginning to gather around, and it looked like a middle-aged woman was preparing to give a speech.

"I forgot about this, we should go over and listen," Larry said. "There was an announcement at the first round of the Tall Tales contest that somebody from the president's office was here to talk about new opportunities on Earth."

"The president of EarthCent is here?"

"His public relations director, and I think I remember reading somewhere that she's his mistress, so she probably speaks for him. I never traded on Earth because it doesn't seem like a promising place to find alien artifacts, but if they make it profitable…"

There was a loud whistle of feedback from the sound system that Fanny's family had rigged to the ship and everybody who still had their high-frequency hearing winced. The woman from EarthCent was obviously an experienced presenter because she didn't flinch or apologize, instead taking advantage of the sudden silence to launch into her speech.

"For those of you who don't read the scandal pages, my name is Hildy Greuen, and I'm here from the president's office to talk about our Twenty-Second Century Bazaar initiative."

"Bizarre?" a kid standing at the bottom of the ramp asked.

"Bazaar, with three A's," Hildy explained. "It's just another name for a trade fair that's permanently in the same place. There's a good example on Flower if any of you get the chance to visit."

"You want us to travel all the way to Earth to lay out our blankets?"

"How many of you are familiar with the concept of subsidies?" Hildy asked in reply.

"You're willing to pay us to come to Earth?" This question put an end to the breakfast conversations that hadn't already been halted, and all heads swiveled toward the woman standing at the top of the ramp.

"Exactly. For some years now, we've been advertising Earth as a tourist destination for aliens, and thanks to the fact that most visitors arrive by passenger liner and take the space elevator, we've had good luck getting them to fill out exit surveys during the long ride back up to orbit. Can anybody guess the most frequent answer to the question about their biggest disappointment after visiting?"

"Air quality," somebody shouted.

"Lack of anatomically correct public restrooms," a wit suggested.

"Crime?" asked one of Fanny's family who was standing behind Hildy.

"All of your answers appeared with some frequency, but the number one complaint was the retail environment," Hildy told them. "Other than the occasional street vendor, the lack of outdoor markets in popular tourist areas is what bothered the aliens most. Many of them said that they would have spent more creds on souvenirs and handicrafts if they'd had the opportunity, but retail stores on Earth are designed for human shoppers and human sensibilities."

"So you want us to travel to Earth to sell local products to aliens?" a trader asked incredulously.

"The first part of the initiative is to fund visiting-trader positions for those of you who are willing to mentor locals in presenting their merchandise and doing business with aliens," Hildy explained. "We'll cover your expenses plus a stipend, and of course, any profits you earn trading on your own account remain yours."

"Talk is cheap," somebody called out. "Where is EarthCent getting the money?"

"They're cleaning up on the All Species Cookbook," another trader in the crowd informed the skeptic. "I just came from Union Station and they can't keep up with the demand. I have two thousand hardcover copies of the Frunge edition if anybody wants to talk business."

"The second part of the initiative, which all of you can take part in even if you have no intention of ever visiting Earth, is telling people about it," Hildy continued. "EarthCent ambassadors are in the process of negotiating deals with the leading travel agencies from all of the tunnel network species. As soon as those agreements are in place, you'll be able to promote low-cost package tours with the Twenty-Second Century Bazaar branding."

"Why would we cut our own throats by sending business to Earth?" an older trader demanded.

"Commission," Hildy responded. "The details have yet to be finalized, but we're hoping to be able to pay five percent of the total value of the tour package as a finder's fee."

"Why?" the same trader asked suspiciously.

"Because advertising is expensive. You don't want to know what twenty-six seconds of commercial time during the broadcast of a Grenouthian documentary costs. And who's in a better position than yourselves to recognize prospects who might be willing to travel to Earth for some shopping? Given the cost and the time commitment required, we're talking about a tiny percentage of your customer base, so you won't be competing with yourselves."

"How is it going to work, the commission thing?" another of Fanny's offspring asked. "Do we have to show up at the travel agency with the prospect?"

"We've licensed a system of unique discount codes from the Drazens," Hildy explained. "It's all handled through your mini-registers, the Stryx take a small percentage. After you sign up at any EarthCent embassy or consulate, your programmable cred will be added to our existing payroll system and you'll be supplied with Drazen coupon blanks. When you have a prospect, you'll enter a null tourism sale into your mini-register which will produce a unique code. Copy that code into the coupon blank, which offers a ten percent discount on the travel package."

"And the commission gets paid to my programmable cred?"

"The travel agencies will remit the code to EarthCent for reimbursement, and the next time you slot your programmable cred into your own mini-register, you'll be paid. If you want to pre-register so we can get an idea of the demand for the coupon blanks, I can take names now."

With that statement, the line for pancakes split like a river that had suddenly discovered a new channel, and half of the people already seated at picnic tables also queued up to supply their contact information for Hildy to enter into her tab.

"Well, that's something," Larry commented to Georgia. "It's probably worth signing up for, but I'll wait until the next time I'm on a Stryx station and do it at the embassy."

"EarthCent must be making even more on the cookbook than I thought," she replied. "Did I tell you my name is in the credits?"

"Miss, uh, reporter," a familiar voice said behind her, and she turned to find Daryl with a woman of around the same age. "This is Kobby. Tell her what you just told me," he instructed his companion.

"I was visiting Earth for the first time last month, and I was approached by a person liquidating a museum collection," Kobby began. "I don't deal in shady goods, I know too many traders who have lost their shirts that way, but this woman had been a curator and she had all of the documentation."

"Do you mind if I record this?" Georgia asked, pulling her reporter's tab from her belt pouch.

"Yes, I mean, no, I don't mind. I want you to publish this. The museum was in a small city, and the curator explained that they had consolidated their collection with another museum in a better location, and she was tasked with selling the leftovers to raise operating cash. I keep most of my money in merchandise, but the deal was so good that I went to the closest MORE branch office. Their reps had introduced themselves to me on Echo Station just a few months earlier, and even though I wasn't interested in a cash-out refi or Advantage, I kept their contact info."

"So you did a mortgage refi and couldn't keep up with the payments?"

"It's worse than that," Daryl put in. "Tell her, Kobby."

"I bought two full sets of armor and spent the rest on swords and other old weapons since I know that the aliens will buy any of that stuff at a premium. I received all of the paperwork showing provenance and everything, but when I arrived here at Aarden, I saw that Flower was in orbit. There's a Frunge blacksmith working at Colonial Jeevesburg on Flower who I've traded with before, so I decided to bring him a few weapons for evaluation."

"Everything was fake," Daryl interjected.

"The blacksmith was very nice about it," Kobby choked out, brushing away a tear with the back of her hand. "He said the replicas were actually very good and offered to take them on consignment to sell to the human gaming fanatics who can't afford real antiques, but they're worth at best a quarter of what I spent on them. I don't know how I'm going to keep up with the new loan payments."

"You'll take me as an apprentice and we'll work on it together," Daryl said.

"Have you reported the fraud to anybody yet?" Georgia asked.

"I showed the paperwork to an expatriate Earth lawyer Flower recommended who lives in the independent living cooperative. Brenda only needed a few minutes to find the small print where everything was identified as museum-quality replicas, including in the provenance documentation. I guess it's something they used to do in small museums on Earth that couldn't afford the real thing. The curator sold them as authentic medieval pieces, but I didn't record my meetings with her, so I don't have a leg to stand on."

"When I file my story, I'll ask the editor to hand-carry it to EarthCent Intelligence since their offices are next door," Georgia said. "I'd like to capture images of the paperwork you received if that's all right with you. Did you have anything else to add?"

"Tell her about the finance manager," Daryl urged.

"That could just be my imagination," Kobby protested. "You know what it's like when you start playing back a conversation in your head."

"But it brings the whole story together."

The woman sighed, and then looked Georgia straight in the eye. "The way I remember it, the finance manager at MORE didn't care what I wanted the money for, she cut me off before I could even explain. She said that my account was in good standing and they'd do a cash-out refi and give me the money to gamble in a casino if that's what I wanted. But when it was all done and I told her I was off to make the biggest purchase of my life, she said, 'Stop worrying. Armor is always a good investment.' It didn't hit me until I got to Aarden and found out I'd been cheated that I never told her I was buying armor."

Eighteen

"I think we're in trouble, Dad," Larry said. "Everywhere I went last night there were people with playing cards in their hatbands buying drinks for the crowd."

"It's my fault, the council's fault, for not seeing this coming," Phil told his son. "We should have realized that as soon as a seat on the council meant more than a lot of drudge work planning the next Rendezvous, candidates with vested interests would get involved. The ironic thing is it will be up to the new council to make any rule changes, and somehow I doubt they'll be shooting the horse they rode in on."

"The two of you sound like a couple of boys whose kite string broke," Rachel scolded them. "Are you just going to give up? You tell them, Georgia."

The freelancer looked up from her tab and then thrust the device at Larry. "Read this," she instructed him, and then proceeded to make it unnecessary by filling everybody in on the contents of the Galactic Free Press article. "The paper ran Ellen's story on the front page. They even hired a Verlock mathematician to provide a forensic statistical analysis of all the Advantage recommendations she documented. He proved beyond a doubt that the platform was designed to create losses."

"You're talking about the new system so many young traders are using?" Phil asked.

"They called it 'Advantage' because it was supposed to give users an advantage over the competition by providing real-time data about market demand. There's a note from the managing editor that while he would have preferred to delay publication until they could identify the responsible parties behind the fraud, the Galactic Free Press believes it to be in the public interest to inform the community now before more traders go broke."

"The reps from the finance outfit that bought my mortgage from the Sharf tried to push some new platform on me right before Joe introduced you back on Union Station," Larry told Georgia. "I didn't hear them out because I wasn't interested."

"Was it MORE?" Georgia asked. "Ellen told me that most of the traders she interviewed first heard about Advantage through MORE financial services, and the name kept coming up with the traders I talked to yesterday."

"Yeah, that's them. I wonder why it's not in the article?"

"Because it would be tantamount to accusing the main servicer of ship mortgages held by humans of trying to drive their borrowers into bankruptcy. We need proof."

"It's possible that the finance company is as much a victim as the traders in this case," Rachel pointed out. "It's doubtful they would know anything about galactic trading conditions, so they're probably just paying the real owners of this Advantage platform to be able to offer clients a benefit."

"It's possible, but it doesn't feel that way to me," Georgia said. "Reporters have a nose for this sort of thing."

"Like you knew Colony One was a scam?" Larry teased her.

"That was different, and Ellen told me that investigative journalists always strike out on their first story. Anyway, read the sidebar by Bob Steelforth, Union Station's chief correspondent. He did an interview with Clive Oxford, the director of EarthCent Intelligence, who said they've launched an investigation into Advantage with the cooperation of Earth authorities and ISPOA, the Inter Species Police Operation Agency."

"Why do I have to read it when you just told me the whole thing?"

"The real question is how this is going to affect the election," Phil said slowly. "It won't have much impact on the older Guild members, but if the majority of young traders with mortgages have been experimenting with the new platform, they're going to be angry."

"But they won't be angry at Larry," Georgia protested.

"They might feel that he represents the establishment that let them down. We'll have to see what the opposition candidates do today—whether they try to connect Advantage with the Conference of Sovereign Human Communities. Even a rumor that humans on a CoSHC world were behind the fraud could be enough to sink us."

"But what would the motive be?" Georgia demanded. "Independent traders are a lifeline for human communities living in space or on alien worlds."

"I think that—" Phil's words were cut off by a 'whomp' sound from somewhere off to the right, and everybody turned in time to see a column of fire ascending to the sky.

Larry knocked over his own coffee jumping up from the breakfast table. "Stay here, Georgia. I'll find out what it is and come back as soon as I can."

"Working press," she retorted, brandishing her credentials at him as she scrambled to get her legs out from under the picnic table. "I'm going with you."

"That was no propane grill going up," Phil called after them. "More likely a fuel pack implosion or an incendiary device."

Before Larry and Georgia reached the site of the explosion, a Vergallian emergency response floater was already overhead, spraying some kind of foam on the remains of a small ship. Larry spotted John standing with Semmi at the edge of the campsite and changed course to meet him. John pointed at his ear to let them know he was talking over his implant, and then a look of relief flooded his face.

"She wasn't on the ship," he said, lowering his hand.

"Who?" Larry asked.

"Ellen. She's still on Flower."

"This was her ship?" Georgia gaped at the foam-covered wreck. "That's horrible. I met her on Flower and we're working together on a follow-up story to her Advantage report. I can message her through my tab to tell her what happened, though I don't know how soon she'll receive it."

"That won't be necessary," John said. "I just spoke to her."

"Your implant can reach into orbit?"

"It only has to reach my ship over there," he explained, pointing off to the side. "I have an emergency Stryxnet relay, one of the perks of my job with EarthCent Intelligence. Ellen took the news in stride, but she said something about just getting out of surgery, so she's probably loaded with painkillers."

"Does this sort of thing often happen at Rendezvous?" Georgia asked.

"First time in my life," Larry told her. "Somebody must not have been happy with that Advantage article, though it's hard to see what they gain from fire-bombing Ellen's ship."

"It tells me that they're afraid of something that hasn't been published yet," John said, running his eyes over the remains of the two-man trader. "This was a professional job. Burning out a Sharf ship on the ground without even scorching its neighbors means a plasma incendiary device with active containment, if not something even more advanced than that."

"Do you mean it wasn't humans?" Georgia asked.

"The technology definitely wasn't human, but the operator could have been. I'm going to talk to the surrounding ship owners and see if any of them had exterior cameras recording, but I doubt I'll learn anything. Whoever did this was professional enough not to get caught."

"I'm going to write a dispatch for the paper," Georgia said. "I'll start interviewing the people here to ask if there are any witnesses. Can you help, Larry?"

"Sure. If I find somebody who saw anything, I'll point them your way."

By the time Georgia and John finished interviewing everybody who was willing to talk, it was almost time for lunch. The job of keeping Semmi amused had fallen to Larry, who discovered that the gryphon was perfectly happy playing fetch, as long as the human did the fetching. As they left the area of the burned-out ship, they found that barriers had been set up to channel everybody to a single exit point. A polite Vergallian soldier asked if they were together and then escorted them into a temporary privacy booth. A uniformed officer sat behind a table

213

next to an impossibly beautiful female who was obviously from the Vergallian upper caste.

"Names?" the officer demanded.

"Larry, no last name."

"Georgia Hunt. Galactic Free Press."

"John, and I'm with EarthCent Intelligence. You can check my programmable cred."

The Vergallian looked at the gryphon expectantly.

"That's Semmi, she's with me," John added. "A Huktra friend left her in my care."

The gryphon snorted at this characterization of the situation, and the upper caste Vergallian who was there to serve as a truthsayer smiled.

"I'll make this as brief as possible," the officer said. "You aren't suspects, but many of the people we've interviewed describe being questioned by a Human intelligence officer or a Galactic Free Press reporter. Did you learn anything that will help us with our investigation?"

"Nobody saw or heard anything of significance," John said. "There must be a connection with the article Ellen just published, but you already know that."

"Somebody who was outside with their kids when the ship went up told me that they didn't even feel the heat, just a sudden change in the air pressure," Georgia contributed. "I've already dictated the story for my paper, though I doubt I'll get more than a couple of lines below the images I took with my implant. Can I get your names for the story?"

The Vergallians exchanged looks, and the officer said, "Not at this time. Did you have a relation to the owner of the ship?"

"I just started working with Ellen two days ago. We interviewed a couple of traders who claimed asylum on

Flower to prevent their ships from being repossessed. She stayed behind to interview more traders about their mortgage financing and have a medical procedure done while I've been doing more interviews down here. She was going to hitch a ride down tonight."

"And you?" the officer asked John.

"We're old friends."

"He's hiding something," the upper-caste Vergallian said immediately.

"When did you last see her?" the officer demanded.

"She pinged me as soon as I landed on Aarden, but we only had a few minutes to talk. Ellen already had a departure ticket for your elevator ground station, and we agreed to get together when she returned."

"That much is true, but he's still hiding something," the truthsayer reported.

"Are you lovers?" the officer inquired.

John hesitated. "We were, many years ago. Ellen was my apprentice but it didn't work out."

"Why?"

"I don't see where that's any of your business."

"A ship has been firebombed on Aarden, the first such occurrence here since your species discovered how to work with copper. Any information potentially related to the incident is our business, and if I'm forced to detain you to get answers to my questions, I will."

"I want you to make a note that I'm answering under protest," John stated. "I'll be filing a complaint through my superior—"

"Do whatever you want on your own time," the officer interrupted. "I see by the yellow ribbon on your arm that you're fond of making speeches, but I really don't have the time."

"My father and uncle were both alcoholics," John said. "It skipped me for some reason, maybe because of what I'd seen, but I've always been one-and-done when it comes to drinks. Ellen is a social drinker."

"He's getting closer," the truthsayer said.

"A heavy social drinker. I couldn't be around it."

"Because you cared about her," the officer stated.

"As a friend."

"He's lying again," the truthsayer reported.

"All right, I loved her, and I couldn't stop myself from nagging her about the booze," John said angrily. "But she didn't believe she had a problem, and for all I know, she might have been right. I couldn't watch her drink even though it's not something that bothered me with anybody else—just her. Satisfied?"

"He's telling the truth."

"What's your story?" the officer asked, peering at Semmi. "Are you with the Human willingly?"

"She says she is, but if she doesn't get something to eat soon, that could change," the upper caste Vergallian said.

"Very well. The four of you can go, but if you learn anything about today's incident, I expect you to inform our security forces immediately."

By the time they got to the improvised dining hall, there were fliers taped to the tent poles showing Larry making a particularly awkward catch above the caption, "Vote for Larry, Semmi's pet."

"I wouldn't worry about it," Georgia reassured him. "Everybody loves the gryphon. It's like an endorsement."

"What bothers me is that our opposition is so organized," Larry said. "How many people and how much money does it take to go from an image capture to a poster on a pole in less than two hours?"

"There's a Vergallian instant print shop set up just outside the Rendezvous grounds," John told him. "I considered getting my own fliers, but I don't have any volunteers to put them up, and it would have been too pathetic to get caught doing it myself."

"The Vergallians sure got to the fire fast," Georgia said. "It couldn't have taken us more than two minutes, but their emergency response ship was already there foaming down the wreckage."

"The campgrounds are temporarily the busiest spaceport on the planet. The Vergallians probably have a full crash team in the area."

"It's part of the contract," Larry informed them. "Whenever Rendezvous is on a planet, the Guild makes sure that the host world provides spaceport-level emergency services. My dad is usually the one who negotiates that stuff and he's been coaching me to take over the responsibility. I don't know what will happen if our opponents win all the seats and take control of Rendezvous."

"If you ask me, the Traders Guild will split in two," John said. "I've talked to more traders about the Conference of Sovereign Human Communities in the last few days than in the decade prior, and I learned that my assumptions were completely off."

"Do you mean the traders have already formed parties without knowing it?" Georgia asked.

The EarthCent Intelligence handler shook his head. "I always thought that the older traders would be the ones against joining CoSHC but I was exactly wrong. It turns out it's those of us who remember visiting sovereign human communities before they were members of a larger group who can really see the difference it's made. The young traders have only heard about the complaints. Down!" John barked at Semmi, who had just plucked the hard-boiled egg out of the salad a woman was carrying back to her table. "Sorry about that."

"You just lost my vote," the woman replied, but her smile belied her words. "You're the EarthCent Intelligence candidate, aren't you?"

"I work for EarthCent Intelligence, but I've also been a trader for most of my adult life."

"We all heard the news about Ellen's ship being fire-bombed. I know it must have to do with her reporting for the Galactic Free Press, but she's a trader too, and we're taking up a collection. You should get up on the stage and say something about it."

John looked longingly at the rapidly dwindling selection of prepared food, but then he nodded his head in agreement. "Can you grab me something, Larry?" he asked. "Better make it triple to feed Semmi or she'll be mooching from everybody again. We'll be back in a minute."

The volunteers working the chow line had been watching the gryphon, and they looked disappointed when she followed John off towards the front of the tent. Georgia noticed their eyes trailing the gorgeous beast and decided to do some mooching of her own.

"You guys wouldn't have any scraps for the gryphon, would you?" she asked. "You know, like something that fell on the ground? From what I've seen, she's not a picky eater."

"There's a half a roast chicken that's about to slide off the tray," the young grill chef insinuated with a wink and pointed at a display of barbequed chickens with his tongs. "It's the one on the end."

"Put it on top of these quality control rejects," the woman working the deep fryer said, and passed Georgia a large box of fries.

"Two more just like that should cover you, me, and John if we share," Larry said to Georgia. "Can you carry a large salad with that? I'll pay the cashier."

"Barb," the grill chef called to the cashier. "A large salad and three chickens in bed, but one of them is a quality control reject for the gryphon."

While Larry was paying at the mini-register with his programmable cred, John reached the event table at the front of the tent and asked if it was possible to patch into the sound system for an announcement about the fund-raiser.

"That wouldn't be fair to the other candidates," the woman in charge said. "Couldn't it wait until the regular speeches tonight?"

"There might be a completely different crowd in here by then," John argued. "Besides, I thought there were no rules."

"He's got a point," a younger trader at the table said, and after a further discussion, they decided to allow him to speak.

The woman in charge had to call for technical support, and by the time a kid arrived and pointed out the menu option on a tab, John was beginning to regret he hadn't stopped to get something to wet his throat. As he began to mount the stage, somebody reached out and handed him a cup of water, making him feel like a marathon runner passing a refreshment station on the racecourse.

A winged blur knocked him off his feet just as he tilted back the cup, and from there, everything got progressively weirder as his vision blurred and went dark. John couldn't feel his limbs, and he wondered for a moment if Semmi had finally let her appetite get the better of her and was gnawing off his legs. There was a strange roaring in his ears that seemed to go on forever, but then he made out Larry shouting something about a stasis pod. The last thing he remembered was a voice talking about somebody's lips turning blue, and then, nothing.

Nineteen

"I quit," Ellen declared, throwing down her cards. "One of you is cheating."

"We're playing for tongue depressors," the giant beetle rubbed out on his speaking legs. "Don't act the spoilsport."

"If you're going to make accusations, be specific," Flower chipped in via the speaker grille of the maintenance bot she had sent to handle the cards for her.

"I didn't want to say anything, but j'accuse," Ellen proclaimed dramatically, pointing at the large pile of tongue depressors in front of the gryphon.

Semmi snorted and motioned with her beak for the Farling doctor to continue the deal.

"Where am I?" John groaned from the operating table.

"He's awake," Ellen cried, leaping up and artistically jarring the wheeled stainless steel medical-instruments table hard enough to scramble the piles of tongue depressors. "Are you all right, John? Can you see me?"

"Of course he's all right," M793qK rubbed out irritably. "He's my patient."

"What happened?" John asked.

"You were poisoned," Ellen told him. "Luckily, there was a group of retirees from the independent living cooperative on Flower visiting Rendezvous and they were eating lunch when it happened. They offered the use of the stasis pod in their shuttle."

"I remember Semmi knocking me down."

"The gryphon saved your life by keeping you from more than wetting your lips. She's hardly left your side since."

"No accounting for taste," the Farling doctor commented. Then he rubbed out something else that John and Ellen's implants failed to translate, but Semmi got up and playfully nipped one of John's toes right through the boot.

"Ouch!"

The Farling buzzed his speaking legs again, and Semmi gently tapped the toe section of John's other boot with the point of her beak.

"Feel that?" M793qK demanded.

"Yes. And I can move everything too. Can I sit up?"

"I don't know. Are you requesting a treat?"

"Play nice, doctor," Flower remonstrated. "The poor man was dead a few hours ago."

"I was dead?" John asked.

"Only in the biological sense—I make no theological assertions," the Farling told him. "Normally I'd charge a thousand creds for detoxification and reanimation, but Captain Pyun was here earlier and told me that EarthCent Intelligence is footing the bill. I'm applying my thirty percent 'friends and foes' discount."

"I remember a guy giving me a cup of water. Did they catch him?"

"Semmi caught him," Ellen said. "I got a message from Georgia that Vergallian security was eventually able to stop the bleeding and they'll move on to interrogation as soon as he's healthy enough. The only thing she knows for certain is that the assassin was a human."

"I could have told you that," John said, pushing himself into a sitting position. "Nobody I recognized, though.

What's this?" he continued, pulling a folded piece of paper out of his breast pocket. "Twenty percent discount on hip-joint replacements?"

"One of the independent living cooperative members must have thought you might have a use for that," Flower commented via the bot's speaker. "Probably Dave. He's always promoting the good doctor's services."

The giant beetle buzzed his speaking legs again, and Semmi pecked John just below the kneecap. His foot flew up and barely missed Ellen.

"That's good enough for me," M793qK said. "You're as healthy as one can expect for a Human."

"Are you sure?" Ellen asked. "Like you said, he was dead just a few hours ago."

"And last night you were a lush. Sometimes I even amaze myself."

"What's he talking about?" John asked. "Is that the elective surgery you mentioned? I thought you were getting the thing on your foot fixed."

"Do you require cosmetic surgery?" M793qK asked Ellen immediately, a gleam coming into his multifaceted eyes. "I offer a quantity discount."

"That was just a bad-fitting pair of shoes," the freelancer responded, "and thank you for violating doctor-patient confidentiality. Did it ever occur to you I might not want everybody knowing the details about my procedure?"

"Doctor-patient what?" the beetle rubbed out. "Surely I mentioned that everything that happens in this office is holographically recorded for training purposes, but I reserve the right to sell it to the Grenouthians if anything amusing happens."

"What's going on, Ellen?" John asked, getting to his feet and taking her hand. "I know I gave you plenty of grief about your drinking but I've seen a lot worse."

"Now you tell me," Ellen complained, but then she shook her head. "You weren't the only one I heard it from, it just took me a few years to believe it. My editor has always supported me, but I could see in his eyes that he thinks I have a problem. Anyway, the doctor says his work can't be reversed."

"I didn't say I can't reverse it," M793qK objected. "I said that I won't reverse it. Even a part-time reporter should be more precise."

"Freelance," Ellen retorted. "And if you're going to split hairs, your exact warning was that if I wanted to start drinking again, I'd have to find another Farling physician who knows as much about primitive biology as you do."

"There aren't any Farling physicians who know as much about primitive biology as I do," the beetle doctor told her. "I thought you would be able to draw that conclusion from the context."

"Did you let him mess with your brain?" John asked, staring into Ellen's eyes.

"The doctor didn't touch my brain," she reassured him. "I came in a couple of days ago and let him take samples from my intestines and he—altered them."

"Altered?" M793qK scoffed. "I completely re-engineered your gastrointestinal tract and I'm applying for a patent. The samples I removed were for experimentation so I could program a swarm of nanobots to make the required changes at the cellular level. I finished deploying the nanobots just before the popsicle package arrived."

"The what?" John asked.

"Stasis pod," Flower explained. "The doctor has a low opinion of Dollnick life-preserving technology. We agreed to disagree."

"You let the Farling poke holes in you to take samples and now he's filled you with Gem nanobots?"

"No scars," Ellen boasted, pulling up her blouse and showing off her abdomen. "And since you're the one who let the cat out of the bag, Doctor, you explain it to him."

"Alcohol enters the bloodstream by way of the gastrointestinal tract," M793qK said. "The nanobots are targeting the glands which excrete the glycosylated proteins that coat the walls of the stomach and intestines to create an alcohol-proof version."

"I don't understand," John admitted.

"That doesn't surprise me. Have you ever gone hiking with those boots on?"

"Sure."

"Do they keep your feet dry in the snow and the mud?"

"They're waterproof."

"And Ellen's mucous will be alcohol-proof as soon as the nanobots finish their work."

John looked from the Farling to Ellen. "So you're going to keep on drinking but you won't get drunk? Somehow, that doesn't seem ideal."

"The re-engineered mucous keeps the alcohol from reaching the capillary system by absorbing it first and immediately beginning passage for evacuation," the Farling said. "The volumetric relationship is approximately ten-to-one."

"You mean, if she tries to drink—"

"I'll be in the restroom all night passing copious amounts of mucous," Ellen said wryly. "The doctor offered me several other options, but they were all worse."

"Welcome back from the dead," the captain said, entering the med bay with a fruit basket. "Compliments of Flower and EarthCent Intelligence."

"Woojin," John greeted him. "I haven't seen you since the last conference on Union Station."

"It's getting awfully crowded in here," the doctor interrupted the reunion. "Why don't you all go and catch up elsewhere, Captain. I have a patient coming in any minute." The Farling buzzed something at the gryphon and added, "You should feed Semmi more protein or her growth spurt might be delayed."

"Growth spurt?" John asked.

"Of course. You didn't think she was an adult, did you?"

"Come, I'll take you to the private cafeteria," the captain said. "Thanks for saving him, M793qK. You know I'm good for the bill."

"I know nothing of the sort," the doctor grumbled.

Woojin led his guests to the nearest lift tube, and then to the small cafeteria that Flower set aside for aliens traveling alone, most of whom had second jobs with the intelligence services of their respective species. "You have a guest on the way," he informed John.

"Who?"

"A Huktra agent named Myort. He parked in Flower's bay just a few minutes ago."

"He must be coming for Semmi," John said, and he was struck by the fact that rather than relief, all he felt was disappointment.

"I don't know about that part, but I have something for you as well," Woojin said, and handed over a ring.

"My poison detection ring. I sure could have used this a few hours ago. Where did you get it?"

"A tough cookie named Liz showed up here while the doctor was bringing you back to life. She said that right after you visited her at the Borten asteroid belt, she found out that the miners being brought into the system were working without proper cosmic radiation shielding and they've started getting sick. Her employer is trying to cover it up, so she smuggled herself out on a supply ship and caught a ride here with a trader coming to Rendezvous."

"Liz gave me a data dump on their operations that I already transmitted to Clive at Union Station," John said. "Is she okay?"

"She wasn't injured, but I don't think she'd slept in days. We gave her a cabin and Flower is keeping an eye on her."

"She's snoring," the Dollnick AI reported.

Semmi began thwacking her tail on the deck when the cafeteria doors slid open to admit Myort, but she remained at John's side. The Huktra winked at his friend, and then produced a chit which he offered to the captain with both hands, being careful to keep the talons from scratching Woojin.

"Greetings from Huktra Intelligence," Myort said. "I've been informed that you are the contact point for all alien intelligence agents stationed on Flower, and although I'm just visiting, I thought it would be appropriate to present my credentials."

"Welcome aboard," the captain responded formally. "I'm afraid I'm not carrying a card to exchange. Clive, I mean, the director of EarthCent Intelligence, told me that you're interested in establishing relations."

"We got the idea from the Drazens," Myort said. "Although your intelligence-sharing relationship with them is somewhat one-sided, your species is up-and-coming, and you do produce the occasional surprising tidbit that the rest of us overlook."

"I didn't know that Drazens and Huktra were on such close terms," Woojin said.

"It's complicated. Our respective leaderships have little interest in official relations beyond the minimum required by the tunnel network treaty, but Herl helped me avoid a serious error some time back, and I've been looking for a chance to reciprocate."

"The director of Drazen Intelligence did you a favor and you want to reciprocate by cooperating with EarthCent Intelligence?"

"Perhaps I should start from the beginning. I've been monitoring certain Drazen communications—"

"You're spying on them?" John interrupted.

"Spying has such a negative connotation," Myort complained. "Let's just say I was sampling some poorly encrypted communications between Drazen businesses on Earth and their field headquarters."

"That's how you're repaying Herl's favor? Remind me not to get on your good side."

"The truth is, favors are dangerous things in our line of work, and Herl would rather keep me in his debt. I merely took the liberty of looking for a way to repay him. If the Drazens want to keep me from reading their correspondence, they should upgrade their technology."

"Which EarthCent Intelligence security is based on," John commented dryly.

"Yes, there's that," Myort allowed. "To make a long story short, I discovered that the Drazen businesses operating on Earth were concerned about the level of criminality and lack of law enforcement in many regions where their

228

suppliers operate, and this was especially the case with Drazen Foods. My own species has yet to establish an official presence on Earth, so I decided to visit and plant a few seeds, if you know what I mean."

"You told me you went to Earth for a restaurant package tour."

"And you believed me? In any case, I was able to pass myself off among your lawless element as a fugitive from justice, and I focused on acquiring sources inside organizations that Drazen Intelligence had flagged for investigation by your Earth law-enforcement."

"You tried to jump the line by hiring informers."

"That's a less elegant way of putting it." Myort produced a standard memory chip and handed it to Woojin. "I'm afraid a holographic recording was beyond my source's ability, but I think you'll find the flat video acceptable in this case."

A panel popped open just to the right of the kitchen door, and Flower instructed Woojin, "Slot the memory in the media interface and I'll project it."

"Never knew that was there," the captain muttered, and after a brief examination, he located the receptacle size that matched the chip. The lights in the room dimmed, and then a grainy image appeared on one of the walls.

"Sorry about the low resolution," Myort said. "My source was attending this meeting undercover and recorded it with a hidden camera in her hairpin."

"I'll do a little interpolation and apply a few filters," Flower said, and the still image improved noticeably. "I could shrink the projection area to sharpen the image further, but I've already skipped ahead and reviewed the contents, and I think you'll find the audio more interesting than the video."

"My source also has some training materials from the presentation that I told her to send to the EarthCent President's office so they can forward it to Union Station in the diplomatic bag," Myort added.

The video began to play, and a friendly man in an expensive suit took his place behind the lectern. "Welcome back to our retraining program," he began. "I'm Gregory, and I'll be handling the afternoon session. I hope you enjoyed your lunch in the executive cafeteria, and if you work hard in the field, you may soon find yourself promoted to management and eating there on a daily basis. All of you should now have a starter kit that includes your business cards, our company manual, a Horten pocket-paralyzer, a company tab, and a checklist for repossessions. Please take a moment to do an inventory and make sure your kit is complete."

"Why does the sign on our building say Triad Financial Services, but according to my business card, I'm a field representative for MORE?" somebody asked.

"I'm glad you noticed," the presenter said, and taking up a stylus, repeated out loud what he printed on the large display panel. "MORE – Make Owners REnters. There, ladies and gentlemen, you have our philosophy in a nutshell. Humanity's progress as a space-faring civilization has been slowed by the stubbornness and inefficiency of our only transportation infrastructure, namely independent traders flying second-hand ships purchased from aliens. It's our goal, or perhaps I should say, our mission, to consolidate the industry in order to improve profitability to the point where we can start working our way up the galactic food chain."

"You're talking about eliminating independent traders," somebody else said.

"Nothing so dramatic. After all, there are millions of them, and while our resources are large, purchasing that many ships is beyond our current means. What we have been able to do is to acquire the majority of outstanding mortgages on Sharf two-man traders. Your job will be to sell refinancing deals to our mortgage customers, with the ultimate goal of enabling us to legally repossess the ships."

"Selling drugs was easier," another attendee complained.

"But we're no longer in the drug business, which means, *you're* no longer in the drug business," Gregory said, and something in his voice made it clear that no argument would be tolerated. "You'll find that offering large sums of money to young traders is actually an easy sell, especially after our special ops team sees to it that your prospects are in need of cash."

The audience, none of whom were visible in the video, broke out in appreciative laughter.

"What's all this promotional material about Advantage?" a woman's voice asked.

"My source," Myort interjected.

"Ah, the pièce de résistance," Gregory said with a broad smile. "Even if your prospects won't sign up for the full refi treatment, you can still earn commissions by getting them to use our free suite of tools that will help increase their profits."

Laughter swelled again, and various voices offered one-word assessments of their marks that were all synonyms for "suckers."

"Can I apply for the special ops team?" somebody asked. "I used to do that sort of thing back home."

"I'm afraid we have all the muscle we need right now, and a shortage of salesmen without prominent tattoos on their faces and hands. By the end of the year, we should achieve our first goal of foreclosing on a quarter of the Sharf ships with outstanding balances, and we'll operate those in such a way to accelerate the losses of the remainder. The traders are a disorganized bunch, and our only fear is that they'll join the Conference of Sovereign Human Communities. We're financing a slate of candidates for the Traders Guild election to make sure that doesn't happen."

The video came to an abrupt end, and Myort said, "Sorry about that, but I bought all of the surveillance gear in a shop on Earth, and the record times on those hairpin cameras is limited. I didn't include the video from the morning session, which was all about the benefits package for the reps. The recording was made almost a month ago and it took that long for the chip to reach me. Earth really does need a better package delivery service."

"This is incredible," Ellen said. "I'm about to publish a follow-up story to my Advantage piece implying a link to MORE based on user testimony, but I was worried my editor might require more proof."

"Will the Galactic Free Press include the video?" John asked her.

"Sure, but if you really want to make sure everybody sees it before the election, offer it to the Grenouthians. Georgia already messaged me everything she has, so I can ask Flower to attach the video and send it all in to the home office. I bet it appears in the paper's next update cycle. You don't have to delay sending the video to the Grenouthians, and the truth is, they're much more likely to run it if they can be first."

"I've forwarded the video to both EarthCent Intelligence and the Galactic Free Press," Flower announced.

"I'm contacting my network source to sell it to the Grenouthians."

"You can just give it to them," John said.

"No, Flower is right," the Huktra told him. "They won't take it seriously unless it comes with a price attached, and the poor video quality is a real drawback for them. Still, I think that they'll run it as a humor piece."

"Lucky for us you were spying on our Drazen allies," Woojin said. "EarthCent Intelligence owes you one."

"I'll owe you two," John said. "I think the election was tilting against us, which would have kept the Guild out of CoSHC."

"I'd like to cash one of those favors in now, if you don't mind," Myort said. "Do you remember what I told you about my wife?"

"Is this the wife who doesn't know she's married to you yet?"

"It's important to project confidence if you want to get anywhere with our females. In any case, she gave me an ultimatum. It's her or the gryphon. So I was wondering…"

"You want me to keep Semmi?" John struggled for a moment with the idea of playing hard to get to use up both of the open favors he'd promised, but the gryphon was looking at him expectantly, so he caved. "As long as she's willing, I'm willing. But you know my ship isn't a quarter the size of yours, and the Farling said that she's due to have a growth spurt."

"I'll put it this way," Myort said. "If you and Ellen live long enough, you'll be able to ride her. Together. At the same time."

Twenty

"Welcome to the last night of Rendezvous, and while I can't promise you the excitement of the last few days, I think you'll all be glad you stuck around until the end," the master of ceremonies addressed the crowd. "Before we proceed to the final round of the Tall Tales contest and the announcement of the election results, a personal representative of the President of EarthCent has an important announcement. Please put down your drinks and your desserts, though for those of you enjoying the complimentary fruitcakes provided by Flower there isn't much difference, and give a warm welcome to the president's mistress, Hildy Greuen."

Even though she looked no larger than an ant to those in the back, the ten thousand plus traders seated at long rows of tables in the enormous Vergallian tent gave EarthCent's public relations director a thunderous round of applause. Hildy climbed onto the stage and took her place at the lectern with the ease of a practiced public speaker.

"Thank you for an introduction that gives new meaning to the phrase, 'Too much information,'" she began. "But in this case, I suppose it's helpful that you all know that I have the president's ear, along with the rest of him. Thanks to Flower's cooperation in providing me with remote Stryxnet access, I just got off a tunneling conference call with the president and the ambassadors of the EarthCent Intelligence Steering Committee."

"If this is a tall tale, it's not funny," somebody called out in a voice that testified to its owner having over-indulged in the alcohol-soaked fruitcake.

"I think those of you with outstanding mortgages on your ships will be glad to hear that I'm not making this up," Hildy responded politely. "You've all read the stories in the Galactic Free Press by now, so you must be wondering about the legal and moral implications of making continued mortgage and refi payments to criminals. While Triad Enterprises, through its MORE subsidiary, was engaged in illegal activities that ranged from predatory lending and the dissemination of false trading information to the sabotage and even destruction of ships, the parent company also draws deposits from legitimate investors. Projectionist?"

A low-quality holographic image of a slowly revolving Earth appeared over the stage.

"Each of those flags you see represents a location where Triad Enterprises has a significant presence providing banking services and employing locals. Given the number of nations and city-states involved, we expect that it will be months, if not years, before the local authorities can untangle the criminal elements from the legitimate business activities and transfer the assets to responsible fiduciaries."

"So do we continue making our loan payments?" a young woman near the stage inquired.

"In short, yes," Hildy said. "Although they aren't tunnel network members, the Sharf government is deeply embarrassed at the unwitting part they played in this criminal scheme. They have instructed their association which handles pre-owned ship sales to other species to buy back all of the securitized mortgages they sold Triad Enterprises, a process that should be completed within days. The payments you submit through your mini-registers will be rerouted to the Sharf, and everything will go back to the way it was in previous years."

"What about the refi deals?" a number of voices called out.

"The situation there is more complicated because of the fraud involved. For the time being, you'll go back to making your original mortgage payments, and when Triad's new management is in place, we'll negotiate a deal that takes the interests of all innocent parties into account. Those of you with refi deals are advised to steer clear of entering Earth's jurisdiction until this is resolved, as repossession counts for nine-tenths of the law."

"Thank you, Hildy," the master of ceremonies said, resuming his place at the lectern. "I didn't understand half of that, but I paid off my mortgage a decade ago so I guess I'm in the clear. Next up we have the finalists in the Tall Tales contest. If you missed any of the preliminary rounds, for a five-cred donation to the Ellen's Ship Fund, you can pick up a recorded chip from the information desk. Without further ado, I give you Trader Yasmine."

"Thank you, Gary," the woman with silver-flecked black hair said, taking her place at the lectern. "No mouse peeking out of the beard this year?"

"Late night, he's sleeping in. You have ten minutes."

"Well, I'll just get started then, though I should caution you all that if you're expecting some wild invention, this is actually a true story about something that happened to me on a Dollnick ag world. I knew from the minute I stepped off my ship that something was rotten, because my monkey, who couldn't be here tonight due to a prior engagement, said to me, 'Yazz, something is rotten.'"

Nine minutes later, the trader wound up the story in which she and her monkey saved the ag world from an invasive species of tuber parasites through a series of coincidences that culminated in her accidental marriage to the Dollnick prince who owned the planet. Yasmine concluded by saying, "I'd love to tell you how I escaped from his four-armed embrace, but time is running out, so I'll have to save that for my soon-to-be-released maiden novel, 'Married to the Trillionaire Alien Prince: Book One.' Buy it wherever they print on demand."

"Thank you, Yasmine, for sharing your harrowing experience with us," Gary said. "It should serve as a cautionary tale for any of you who frequent Dollnick ag worlds on business, as forewarned is forearmed."

There were loud groans from the crowd, and not a few traders could be heard repeating the bad pun while waving four fingers in the faces of their neighbors and explaining, "Forearmed is four-armed, you idiot. Get it now?"

"Next up is Darla, who recently returned from trading among the pirates on the Horten frontier," Gary said. "Darla, you have ten minutes."

"The last time a man said that to me, he was grossly overestimating his stamina," the willowy trader said as she took her place behind the lectern. "Like Yasmine, I'm going to disappoint those of you who are expecting a tale out of a Vergallian drama. Everything I'm about to tell you really did happen to me, and if it wasn't for good luck and the intensive training I received as an orphan raised by Horten assassins, I wouldn't be here today."

There were audience members running for the portable toilets by the time Darla wrapped up the story in which she prevented a pirate invasion of the tunnel network by teaming up with a young Stryx who was tired of doing multiverse math homework. Together they opened a rift in the space-time continuum and sent the attack fleet into an alternate universe, where the would-be invaders all accepted highly compensated work as reenactors at pirate-themed resorts.

"If any of you doubt a word of it, and I couldn't help seeing the skepticism on some faces when I related how I was beheaded, you're welcome to come up here after the voting and inspect the scar," she concluded, drawing an index finger across her neck.

"Thank you, Darla," the master of ceremonies said, tilting his head to inspect her neck as she passed, but his eyes strayed lower. She yanked on his beard in response, and a small grey mouse popped out and scolded everybody in sight. It took almost two minutes for Gary to calm the creature sufficiently to continue.

"Our final contestant is Marshall, who some of you will remember as last year's runner-up with his true story about being swallowed by a Floppsie while space-walking to fix a weather-control satellite for a primitive civilization which mistook him for a Terregram mage after he had been tarred and feathered at his previous stop. Marshall?"

"Thank you for reducing my epic tale of suffering and redemption to a fifteen-second highlight reel," Marshall said as he assumed his place behind the lectern. "Unlike the other contestants tonight, I'm going to do something different this year and spin you a tale of which not a single word is true. It all started a little over a month ago on Earth, when a trader I'd never met before passed by my blanket cursing like a sailor at her twentieth-generation cell phone, which for those of you who don't know, is what passes for personal communications technology on our motherworld."

Marshall went on to tell the story of how Ellen had conducted her investigation of Advantage and MORE, with certain embellishments, such as admitting that he was the undercover operative who had obtained the damning video, and insinuating that Ellen had remained on Flower for several days because he warned her of an assassination plot.

"Thank you, Marshall," Gary said, giving the older trader a wink as they exchanged places. "I especially liked the part where you convinced your old friend, President Beyer, to send his mistress along with Ellen as a human shield, because after all, who would risk incurring the wrath of EarthCent?"

"I get around," Marshall replied modestly, and took his seat on the remaining folding chair.

"So the time to vote for the Tall Tale Teller of the year is upon us. If you'll get out your tabs and head to the main screen for Rendezvous, you'll find it's been replaced with the names of our three contestants in the order in which they performed. You can only tap one name before the screen locks out, so take a minute to think, and while you're doing that, our outgoing council head has a special announcement. Phil?"

Larry's father, who had been waiting at the event table, climbed onto the stage and took Gary's place at the lectern. "I'll keep this brief and try not to steal anybody's thunder," he said. "I'm sure you're all aware that this year was the first time we had a competitive election for council seats rather than me having to chase around drafting volunteers.

239

I want to thank all of the candidates for participating. A few hours ago, I was approached by the young traders running on an anti-incumbency platform, among other things, and they all requested that their names be removed from consideration."

"Good riddance to them," somebody shouted. "Those free cards were all marked."

"They wanted to stress the fact that they believed their financial backers were acting in good faith, and they didn't know about MORE's scheme to become the dominant force in independent trading. They also didn't know that the decks were marked. Mountain Man Gary will be announcing the election results immediately after the winner of the Tall Tales contest accepts his or her prize, and I want to take this final opportunity to thank you for your votes over the last thirty years. Gary?"

"And the results are in," the master of ceremonies declared, looking down at his own tab. "The winner is Marshall with his thoroughly unbelievable tale about corruption in the financial services industry. Darla is this year's runner up, and Yasmine, I loved your story, but I think you lost a few points with the book plug at the end. Marshall?"

The older trader approached the lectern and accepted the trophy featuring a figurine which had one hand behind its back with the fingers crossed. "I've been trying to win this damn thing for more years than I can remember," Marshall said, and his voice choked up with real emotion. "I want to thank Ellen for letting me borrow what is really her story, and to say that I'm donating the winner's purse of one thousand creds to the Ellen's Ship Fund so she's not left paying a mortgage on a pile of slag."

"Insurance?" a few voices shouted.

"The Tharks have an exclusion for damage caused by vandalism or the fire-bombing of ships in use by working press and intelligence agents," Marshall said. "I'm told that with the donations collected so far, we're still around six thousand creds short of paying off the mortgage, and that doesn't even touch on her lost equity. I think the trading community owes her at least that much. Thank you all for making me the Tall Tale Teller of the year, even if it's only because I went last and was fresh in your memories when you voted."

"Thank you, Marshall," Gary said. "I see some people getting up to leave, so I'll just hurry up and say that the incumbents for the Traders Guild Council were all returned to their seats, with the exception of Arlene, who didn't make it here in time to register. Her place will be filled by Semmi's John, and Phil's seat as the council's head has been successfully passed to his son, Larry, who will say a few words."

The tent really started emptying out in earnest as Larry took the stage, and he began speaking the moment he reached the lectern. "I'll skip the formalities and just say that the older council members have appointed me to be our representative to the Conference of Sovereign Human Communities because none of them wanted the job and John is too busy with his EarthCent Intelligence work. But I want to take the opportunity in front of those of you who are still here to ask, Georgia? Will you be my apprentice?"

"He just proposed in trader terms," Ellen said, jabbing the younger journalist with her elbow. "Say something."

"Yes," Larry's mother called out, and then turned to Georgia. "This way it's not legally binding and you can always change your mind after taking him out for a test drive."

The next morning, Larry and Georgia met Ellen and John at the latter's ship. The two reporters went to work on a wrap-up piece about Rendezvous, while the men tried to get the better of each other trading merchandise from their stock that hadn't moved for years.

"You'll make a killing with these socks next time you visit Verlock space," Larry promised the older man. "The only reason I'm letting them go is that I want to do a circuit of the CoSHC worlds I haven't visited yet in preparation for the convention."

"There are at least a half-dozen Verlock open worlds with academies in the Conference of Sovereign Human communities," John pointed out skeptically.

"I've been to them already trying to buy used magnetic monopoles." Larry pulled one of the socks onto his arm and spread his fingers in a 'V' with the thumb stretched to the side. "Three toes, you can't miss."

"It's not that I don't want the socks," John said, and changed over to a honeyed tone. "It's that I follow a strict rule about apportioning my cargo and I'm full up on clothing and accessories. Now, if you'd take a gross of Grenouthian hats in exchange…"

"I've never seen a Grenouthian in a hat," Larry said suspiciously. "What makes them special?"

"The ear holes. But you could always patch those and then they'd be good for any species with big heads."

"Do they stack?"

Semmi got tired of listening to the men who were all talk and no action and decided to get in some exercise before the ship took off. She gave a loud "Caw," to get everybody's attention, and scratched out a perfect circle with her right front paw. Next, she used her beak to add two lines of different lengths, and then took to the sky.

"What was that about?" Georgia asked.

"It's one of the ways Semmi communicates," John said, going around and standing where the gryphon had been when she scribed the lines. "The big hand is straight up and the little hand is ninety degrees down, so I'd say she'll be back at three this afternoon."

"Is she really that smart?" Larry asked.

"Smart enough to cheat at poker," Ellen said. "The Farling doctor told me that she's smarter than most humans he's met, but Flower claimed he says that about everybody's pets. Why don't the two of you take a break from trying to out-trade each other and make us lunch?"

"Are you almost finished?" John asked.

"Georgia is just adding a bit about the new foods she discovered at this Rendezvous, and I'm going to write a few words about Marshall's win and the results of the fundraiser. It feels a little weird to be reporting on a charity for myself, but it's part of the story, and the Galactic Free Press already offered to make good any losses that the collection didn't cover."

"Come on, Larry," John said. "I'll show you my stock of freeze-dried rations and break a few open for lunch so you can get a sample before you buy."

"Who says I'm buying?"

"Put them on my tab," Georgia said. "Ellen told me about those rations, so get us two of each, and I'll have something to write about."

"I hope you're not giving up on investigative journalism," Larry said. "I know you got off to a rough start with the Colony One thing, but your editor has to take you seriously after all the stories you've had published the last week."

"Ellen says it's always a good idea to have some any-time stories in the bank, and food is my go-to fallback."

The introduction of freeze-dried meals to the trading forced Larry to start offering merchandise that he wouldn't have just as soon given away to make space. By the time the men concluded the deal and actually rehydrated a few packets, the women had finished their stories and everybody ate lunch.

"Where does Semmi go when she flies off like that?" Georgia asked.

"I just hope she's not hunting," John said. "Aarden is pretty built-up, and I'm sure that the farmers wouldn't take kindly to a gryphon raiding their flocks."

"They've probably never seen one before," Larry said. "Where are you headed next?"

"I've got to return to the Borten system to follow up on some EarthCent Intelligence business, and Ellen should get a story out of it as well. By the time that wraps up, we'll probably have to head for the Sol system so she can do her Earth Syndication Coordinator thing."

"So the two of you are partnering up?" Georgia asked.

"I'm too good for him, but with my ship destroyed and the pre-owned market being in a mess, I'm kind of stuck," Ellen said.

"Well, it's been a fun week, but if I don't spend some time with my parents before they leave, my mom will kill me so dead that even a Farling doctor won't be able to bring me back," Larry said, rising from the table. "I'll keep the council posted about my progress with CoSHC, John, but you're probably the only one who will read it."

"And I've learned so much from you in just a few days," Georgia said to Ellen. "Anytime you need another pair of feet on a story, tell Roland you want me."

"Will do," Ellen said, and got up to exchange a brief hug. "Take care of yourselves."

John began breaking down the campsite as soon as Larry and Ellen were on their way. "Nice young couple," he commented. "We'll give Semmi until three-fifteen, and if she doesn't show —"

"We'll wait until she does," Ellen interrupted. "We don't need an angry gryphon chasing us around the tunnel network. Speaking of which, do I get added to your ship controller, or are you and Semmi going to treat me like a second-class citizen?"

"I can't speak for the gryphon, but when it comes to adding you to the controller, it's not going to happen."

Ellen's face fell, but she affected a light tone and said, "Letting the beetle doctor rejigger my intestines so I can't drink any more wasn't enough for you?"

"I can't add you to the controller because I never took you off."

"I forgot what a jerk you can be," she said, slipping an arm around his waist and fisting him in the ribs.

"Welcome home."

Freelance on the Galactic Tunnel Network could have been the eighteenth book of my **EarthCent Ambassador** series, but I decided to spin it off since it doesn't include the EarthCent ambassador. I wrote this book so that it doesn't contain too many spoilers about Union Station, and readers who haven't read that series can start with the discounted three-book bundle, **Union Station 1, 2, 3**.

If you like science fiction without wars, you should also enjoy my **EarthCent Universe** series, which starts with **Independent Living**, and the stand-alone **AI Diaries** trilogy, which starts on present day Earth with **Turing Test**. You can sign up for e-mail notification of my new releases on the **IfItBreaks.com** website or find me on Facebook.

About the Author

E. M. Foner lives in Northampton, MA with an imaginary German Shepherd who's been trained to bite central bankers. The author welcomes reader comments at e_foner@yahoo.com.

247

Made in the USA
Las Vegas, NV
05 September 2022

54660351R00146